Cathy Williams can remember reading Mills & Boon books as a teenager, and now that she is writing them she remains an avid fan. For her, there is nothing like creating romantic stories and engaging plots, and each and every book is a new adventure. Cathy lives in London. Her three daughters—Charlotte, Olivia and Emma—have always been, and continue to be, the greatest inspirations in her life.

Also by Cathy Williams

Seduced into Her Boss's Service
A Virgin for Vasquez
Snowbound with His Innocent Temptation
Bought to Wear the Billionaire's Ring
The Secret Sanchez Heir
Cipriani's Innocent Captive
Legacy of His Revenge
A Deal for Her Innocence

Discover more at millsandboon.co.uk.

A DIAMOND DEAL
WITH HER BOSS

CATHY WILLIAMS

MILLS & BOON

First Published in Great Britain 2018
by Mills & Boon, an imprint of HarperCollins*Publishers*
1 London Bridge Street, London, SE1 9GF

© 2018 Cathy Williams

ISBN: 978-0-263-93447-2

Printed and bound in Spain
by CPI, Barcelona

To my three wonderful and inspiring daughters.

CHAPTER ONE

'You're late.' Gabriel pushed himself away from his giant walnut and steel desk to look at the small, dark-haired woman moving briskly to pull out a chair so that she could position herself in front of him.

She was clutching her laptop under her arm and carrying a flat white coffee in her free hand, bought on her way in from a mobile one-man-band seller of excellent coffee who had set up camp outside the towering glass building that housed Gabriel's headquarters.

So far, so good.

Except it wasn't eight-thirty, her usual time of arrival. Nor was it nine-thirty. In fact, it was after ten, which was definitely out of the ordinary. Gabriel looked at his watch significantly, catching her eye as she glanced up at him.

'I know.' Abby could barely meet his gaze as she carefully rested his coffee on his desk and sat in front of him. On the outside, she was as serene and composed as she always was. It was part and parcel of having to deal with the adrenaline-charged, volatile personality of her boss. Anything less than serene wouldn't have made it past the six-month mark and she had been his PA now for over two years.

On the inside, however, she was a nervous wreck because she was about to shake the foundations of Gabriel's carefully composed life and he was not a man who took kindly to having his foundations shaken.

'So?' Gabriel vaulted to his feet, eyebrows raised, every sniffer instinct on full alert, because if there was one thing that could be said about his secretary, it was that she was the very essence of efficiency predictability. He couldn't think of the last time she had arrived late. No, he could, and the answer was *never*. 'Don't leave me in suspense.' He grinned and approached her in ever-decreasing circles until he was towering right beside her.

'You know what a crashing bore I am,' he murmured. 'I loathe anything out of the ordinary.'

Abby could recognise a back-handed piece of self-congratulation when she heard one because the one thing no one could accuse Gabriel of being was a *bore*. And he knew it.

Momentarily distracted from the business at hand, she looked at him with a touch of exasperation but, as always, direct contact with Gabriel's darker-than-night eyes left her feeling a little breathless and frazzled. Abby didn't belong to that long, long queue of glamour women between the ages of eighteen and eighty who went weak at the knees the second Gabriel looked in their direction, but he still managed to have an effect on her which she had long since learned to ignore.

'Would you mind sitting down?' She arched her eyebrows, keeping all outward signs of her lack of composure under wraps. Her boss was eagle-eyed when it came to spotting the tiniest of reactions in other people and he was fond of pouncing. Abby wanted to say what she had to say before any pouncing had a chance to take place. 'You're giving me a crick in my neck.'

'So?' He perched on the edge of his desk, still too close but at least no longer towering. 'Why the departure from your usual routine? Unexpected dental appointment? Sick cat in urgent need of a vet? Crashing hangover?' Gabriel didn't object to a little unpredictability and variety in his private life although, in fairness, variety was now a thing of the past given the fact that he was a man travelling at speed towards the altar.

However, in his professional life, unpredictability was not something he encouraged and he hoped his trustworthy secretary wasn't going to start becoming unpredictable. That would pose a number of problems, the main one being that he couldn't envisage having such a successful working relationship with anyone else. Something about her calm complemented the aggressive energy of his personality, grounded him in ways he had become accustomed to.

He paled because on top of the sick pet, emergency tooth filling and oversleeping her alarm came another, more likely possibility.

'You're not...are you?'

'Not what?'

'I don't even know if you have a boyfriend. You've worked for me for over two years and I still don't know whether you have a boyfriend or not.'

'What has that got to do with anything?' Abby flushed and bristled.

'Most bosses know at least some details of their PA's private lives! You're so secretive, Abby. Why are you so secretive?'

'Gabriel, I honestly have no idea where this is going.'

'If I'd known that there was a man lurking in the background, then I might have braced myself for the inevitable.'

Abby looked at him in open confusion. Gabriel's brilliant mind had a disconcerting habit of whizzing around in unexpected directions until, hey presto, he got precisely where he wanted to be, leaving the rest of his competition miles behind and breathless, but even for him this line of deduction was bewildering.

'Inevitable?'

'Simple process of deduction: you're never late… so I'm assuming something unexpected has reared its ugly head, or else you're not well. Yet here you are! So…temporary bout of sickness? Maybe a trip to the doctor? I'm joining the dots here…'

His dark eyes zeroed in on her flat stomach and Abby felt her muscles contract and tense. Then she felt something else, an *awareness* that made her breathe in sharply, because it crashed through the protective layers she had built around herself, layers that safeguarded her against the dynamism and virility of her impossibly sexy boss.

'What dots are you joining? I'm not pregnant!' she exclaimed impatiently. 'And the reason I don't talk about my private life isn't because I'm secretive—it's because it's actually none of your business, Gabriel!'

'That's called secretive,' Gabriel pointed out without batting an eye. 'Women always like to talk about their private lives.'

Abby gritted her teeth with a distinct lack of the cool reserve of which she was so proud.

'But I can't say that I'm not relieved.' He was carrying on now with considerable less tension. 'And I want to tell you right now that you should never be hesitant about telling me if and when you fall pregnant. I don't belong to that category of male chauvinists who think that a woman with a child is a liability in the work place.'

'Equality has come a long way since the Dark Ages.' Abby had no idea how her simple speech had managed to become so derailed but then she realised that she hadn't actually been allowed to get a word in.

'You'd think so, wouldn't you?' Gabriel smirked. 'Trust me when I tell you that I know otherwise.' He paused. 'So, you still haven't said why you're late.'

'I...er... Gabriel, I was out last night...' This was hardly the crisp speech she had mentally rehearsed on her way to the office, but she hadn't foreseen a hijacking of her prepared agenda by her unpredictable boss. 'I went to a club, in actual fact.'

'A *club*? On a *Thursday*?'

'Yes, Gabriel! It's actually not that unusual. In fact, the club was packed. Because people do that—they *go to clubs*. Even *on Thursdays*!' But Abby knew that she was red as a beetroot and getting more flustered by the second when she thought about what had taken her out of her comfort zone to the club. An Internet date. Rather, someone she had met on a dating app who had seemed very promising at the start of the evening, when they had been having a tame drink at a very civilised bar in the city. True, she had had to resist glancing at her watch every so often, and had had to keep reminding herself that after two years of celibacy it was high time she jumped back into the dating pool, but even so...

Well, he hadn't been an ogre. Nice looking, wire-rimmed specs and a suit and a decent job at a large accountancy firm.

There'd been no reason for her *not* to go to the club with him. How was she to know that after four hours what had started out as nice enough would develop into *interminably dull*?

Maybe that was why she had started looking around her. The music had been loud and she had had a few minutes' reprieve while he had braved the crowds at the bar to replenish their drinks, ignoring her protests that it was time she went home.

The outfit she had chosen to wear, something that shrieked 'smart bar' and definitely not 'hip club', had been uncomfortable and itchy in the overheated, dark room, and people-watching had been a distraction to stop herself from jettisoning her date and sprinting to the nearest exit.

She hadn't expected to recognise anyone. She didn't mix with people who went to clubs. In fact, her circle of friends was tiny and limited to the girls she played tennis with once a week and a handful of university friends who spent more time planning to get together than actually getting together.

It had been hot, it had been dark but she hadn't been able to miss Lucy, Gabriel's fiancée. How could you miss someone with waist-long white-blonde hair, legs that went on for ever and a body that made men stop in their tracks and do a double-take?

Lucy Jackson was a catwalk model with the sweetest of personalities and, not only had Abby been shocked to see her dancing with abandon in a club, she had been even more shocked to see her getting more than a little comfortable with a guy who was as beautiful as she was.

Shock had given way to confusion and then anger because how on earth could she do that to Gabriel?

She'd spent so long staring in horror that it had been little surprise that Lucy had half-turned and caught her eye. For the following hour, Abby had almost wished herself back with the interminably boring accountant, because a tearful Lucy had cornered her and dragged her off to the quietest spot in the nightclub, where the sound from the music was still so loud that Abby had been able to feel her brains rattling around in her head.

'I *thought* I could marry Gabriel!' Lucy had half-wept. 'It's not that I don't *care* about him, but…he's just *not* my type. Mummy and Daddy were so *happy* when he proposed but I just *can't*… He's so…so…*serious*, always *working* and stuff…'

Abby had bit down the very natural retort that sprawling technology empires that raked in billions every year didn't get that way under the guiding hand of someone who holidayed and partied all year long.

'I *wish* you hadn't seen…*you know*…' Lucy had chewed her lip anxiously but then had brightened. 'But Rupe really *gets* me. He's a model like me and he doesn't get all funny about *having a good time*. I *know* he's not eligible like Gabriel, and honestly, Abby, Daddy's going to *kill* me, but I just can't go through with it. Now you know, please, please, *please* could you tell Gabriel? He's going to go *mad* and I know I'll just cave in because I *hate* making a fuss…'

Abby had been appalled.

'Tell him?' she had bellowed above the bass beat of the music. 'Lucy, are you *mad*?' But sweet-natured Lucy had proved that everyone had a mulish side. She had dug her heels in, pleaded and begged, shed some tears and Abby had cracked.

Which didn't make it any easier now, standing here having dragged her boss back from his wild speculations.

She took a deep breath and said casually, 'You'll never guess who I bumped into at the club.'

Gabriel looked at her narrowly. 'I'm sensing we're getting to the heart of the matter now,' he said drily. 'So, instead of going round the houses, why not just spit it out?' He spread his arms wide in a gesture of benevolent magnanimity. 'I think you'll find that I'm pretty unshockable when it comes to finding out what happens in clubs. There's a very good reason I stopped frequenting all but my private one.'

Abby was aware that time was passing. Gabriel, workaholic that he was, didn't seem unduly bothered but there were never sufficient hours in the day for her and she wasn't enthusiastic about hanging around until late in the evening, having been the messenger of bad tidings. She had no idea how Gabriel was going to take what she had to tell him but she foresaw an uncomfortable day ahead for herself.

'I saw Lucy there.'

'Fiancée Lucy?'

'The same.' She looked at him, head cocked to one side.

'If you're expecting me to have a jealous meltdown,' Gabriel inserted wryly, 'Then you'll be waiting a long time. Lucy is her own person and, if she wants to go to a nightclub, then she's more than welcome to do that.' He was momentarily distracted as he wondered who Abby had gone to the nightclub with. A band of women, all drinking cocktails and dancing around handbags? Had she gone there to pick a man up? Surely not? But *why* not? She was in her mid-twenties and, whilst she might dress like someone twice her age, there was something captivating about her face.

Gabriel took a couple of minutes to dwell on what it was that seemed to hold one's attention for a little longer than was strictly necessary. It wasn't as though she was beautiful. Lucy was beautiful, he thought absently, with her tall, rangy body and her long blonde hair. Abby's looks ran to unusual, intelligent, characteristics that shouldn't set the imagination alive with curiosity but somehow did.

She had shoulder-length dark hair which was usually tied back and grey eyes fringed with surprisingly lush lashes and well-defined brows. And her mouth was *sexy*. It wasn't the first time Gabriel had clocked that about his very efficient, very controlled and deliberately in-the-background secretary, but it was the first time he wasn't controlling his imagination—and maybe that was because he was now picturing her in a club. A hot, sweaty, noisy club surrounded by gyrating bodies in skimpy clothing.

Involuntarily, his dark eyes roved over her body. As always, she was neatly turned out in a white blouse, a grey, knee-length skirt and flat, black, sensible pumps. Just the sort of get-up most self-respecting twenty-something women would have flung to the back of their wardrobes. In his mind's eye, however, he was seeing a cropped top, a short skirt and high heels...in flamboyant colours.

Aware of the direction of his gaze, Abby went bright

red and adjusted her skirt primly. 'Lucy wasn't there on her own,' she began.

'Who were you there with?'

'I beg your pardon?'

'Who did you go with? You're normally so reserved when it comes to talking about yourself that I expect you can understand my curiosity now.'

'No, I can't, Gabriel,' Abby told him flatly. 'And if you'd stop interrupting me and allow me to continue...'

'What does my fiancée have to do with you arriving late for work this morning?'

'We spent a good part of the evening talking and I ended up getting home far later than I'd anticipated, hence I overslept. That's why I'm late. And I overslept because I was up most of the night following our conversation.'

'You're talking in riddles.'

'Lucy was there with a guy, Gabriel, someone called Rupert. I hate saying this, and I know that I should never have been tasked with saying it, but I promised so here goes: Lucy is having cold feet about the marriage. She was at the club with this man and they were obviously...somewhat intimate.'

Gabriel's dark eyes flicked to her face and he stilled because this was hardly what he'd been expecting to hear. From anyone else, he might have wondered whether they were having him on or else overplaying something relatively innocent but, coming from his PA, those two options were ruled out immediately.

'I'm sorry,' Abby said huskily. 'This isn't something I want to be doing right now, but Lucy left me with little choice.'

'Rupert.'

'It would be far better if the two of you sat down and had a conversation about this without me in the middle being used as a go-between.'

'So my fiancée is screwing someone else.'

'I never said that!'

'The implication is there.' He clenched his jaw and strolled towards the vast pane of glass that occupied one side of his office and overlooked the city.

Hand thrust into his trouser pocket, he stared out, barely registering the busy streets several storeys below.

He should be gutted, devastated and raging with a desire to hit something or someone—Rupert at the very least, a guy he vaguely knew. Or maybe a brick wall. Something upon which he could vent his anger.

Actually, all he felt was a certain amount of disappointment. *The best laid plans,* he thought.

He felt Abby touch him gently on his shoulder and he spun round to register the concern on her smooth, oval face.

'I'm very sorry,' she said quietly. 'I think Lucy was anxious that you would be angry with her.'

'So she thought she would use you as the middle man to diffuse some of my anger?'

'I guess so. She really does like you, Gabriel. She just isn't sure that you're the one for her, or at least that was what she told me. I wouldn't normally have this conversation but she was desperate for me to pass on the message.'

'How thoughtful of her. Since I appear to be having a break-up by proxy, what reasons did she give?'

Abby marvelled at how well he was managing to rein in all emotion. His personality was so forceful, so unapologetically alpha male, that his composure at a time when he should have been tearing down the office was disconcerting to say the least. Not that she wasn't relieved, because she was.

Relieved and suddenly curious.

Curiosity, however, wasn't part of the package when it came to being Gabriel's PA. Abby liked to keep her working life in one box and her private life, what little there was of it, in another.

'I don't think she liked the thought of marrying someone who spends most of his time working.'

'Understandable.'

'I guess in her profession, she goes out a lot, to parties and so on and so forth, and she couldn't envisage you accompanying her to them.'

'Definite point there.'

'I guess she thinks she might end up with someone who isn't fun.'

'No one can deny that I enjoy work,' Gabriel murmured, 'Although I'm hurt that I'm seen as someone who can't have fun.'

'Gabriel, you don't seem too…too…upset by this. She's your *fiancée*! You must be breaking up inside.'

'I like to imagine that I'm a resilient sort of guy, and it has to be said that it's better that doubts cast their long shadow before the vows are taken rather than the other way around. Wouldn't you agree?'

'Yes, but…'

'You want to see me weeping?' he questioned coolly and with such self-control that Abby blushed.

She was no romantic. She'd been through the mill and had emerged with a healthy amount of scepticism when it came to flowers, chocolates and fairy-tale endings, but she now realised that she might have downplayed her own fundamental belief that happy-ever-afters existed.

'It's none of my business how you react or don't react.' She shrugged, back to her normal cool. 'I didn't want to do this but Lucy left me very little choice. I'm sure you'll want to get in touch with her yourself and pass the message on. I just thought that… Of course, I didn't expect you to weep…'

'My grandmother,' he said succinctly, surprising himself, because for all his outwardly easy banter he, like the woman standing in front of him, was intensely private and was seldom lured into revealing more than he wanted to. Yet here he was…

'Your grandmother?' Abby frowned. She'd taken a surreptitious step back but she was still so close to him that she could feel his heat and the energetic, physical dynamism of his personality. He dwarfed her and very occasionally made her so intensely aware of her femininity that she had to fight to retain her self-control.

It was happening right now as he stared down at her with unfathomable dark eyes.

It never failed to puzzle her how someone could wear the most expensive of business suits yet manage to look nothing like a conventional businessman.

'My grandmother has suffered a series of mini strokes,' Gabriel said, as serious as she had ever seen him. 'They have taken their toll. Despite the fact that she's been given a clean bill of health, she has become depressed about her future, and vocal about her sadness at not seeing me settled with a nice wife who will bear me nice kids and look after me in my dotage.'

'Okay…' Abby was shocked at this admission, which took them veering wildly off the employer-employee road they were accustomed to travelling down. Perhaps this was his vulnerability being exposed, she thought, acknowledging that alongside her surprise was a certain illicit thrill that he was confiding in *her*. 'What about your parents, Gabriel?'

'Both dead.' He lowered his eyes and kept to himself the recognition that, like his grandmother, his father and mother, who had enjoyed a wonderful, close marriage, likewise had been disappointed in him. First his mother, who had died leaving his father bereft, and then his father who, Gabriel often thought, had died from a broken heart, unable to cope with the fact that sudden illness had stripped him of his childhood sweetheart.

'I'm so sorry.'

'It was a long time ago. The fact is that I was effectively raised by my grandmother. It pains me that her one wish, to see me settled, has gone unfulfilled.'

'Hence you decided to get married to Lucy.' There was no need for her to add *before it's too late*. 'But what about love?'

Gabriel looked at her with brooding amusement, the handsome lines of his lean face sending a rush of awareness through her body. This was the most personal conversation they had ever had and, whilst Abby told herself that she couldn't wait to return to the business of work, she was alarmed at how much she was enjoying this rare insight into her boss's thought processes.

She'd met a number of his girlfriends in the past. Sexy, confident women who knew what effect they had on the opposite sex and enjoyed playing to an audience. So why Lucy out of all of them? Abby was ashamed at the pull of curiosity and she looked away.

'I am no great believer in that particular emotion,'

Gabriel drawled, then he grinned and murmured in a low, silky voice, 'But I'm beginning to think that you might be.'

'Then you'd be wrong,' Abby blurted out.

For a few seconds time stood still as their eyes tangled and a slow drumbeat pounded inside her, drying out her mouth and scrambling her thoughts.

'Poor Lucy,' she snapped, pulling back and giving herself time to get her act together under a show of antagonism.

'Because she had the misfortune to have worn my diamond on her finger?' Gabriel was amused and vaguely aware that he was picking up vibes that were quite unlike anything he had felt before in his PA's presence. 'Many women would have been delighted.'

'Perhaps you should have chosen one of them.'

'Wouldn't have worked.' He grinned, inviting her to ask the inevitable, but of course she stubbornly refused to, so he added, anyway, 'Lucy and I go back a little way and there's one thing compelling in her favour: she comes from just the right background.'

Abby wondered why that felt like a slap in the face. 'I had no idea that sort of thing mattered to you, although of course it's none of my business.'

'No, it's not,' Gabriel purred in agreement. 'But now that the door's been opened, so to speak, I'd rather you're not left with any stones unturned. Naturally, I'll get in touch with Lucy, but she's mistaken if she imagines I'm going to give her a hard time. She'll get enough of that from her parents. No, I shall give her my blessing for her future life with the chinless wonder, Rupert. And, to satisfy your curiosity, I don't care what anyone has or doesn't have but, when it comes to the business of marriage, it makes sense to tie the knot with a woman who isn't in it for the money.'

Abby thought of some of the women she had met— flamboyant, seductive and definitely not out of the top drawer.

He had said that he'd wanted to satisfy her curiosity but she discovered that, instead, he had awakened it and that dismayed her.

'Now,' he drawled, pacing the spacious office to take up residence in front of his desk, all business now in record time, 'Down to work.' He paused and looked at Abby as she slowly made her way to her usual position at her desk in front of him, ready for the day to begin, albeit later than was customary. 'She should not have put you in the position she did,' he said seriously.

'She's young.'

'Which is something I failed to take into account,' Gabriel conceded wryly. 'That, along with the fact that she expected rather more than was on offer, even though by anyone's standards what was on offer was a pretty good deal.' He stared thoughtfully off into the distance. 'Now there's just the business of breaking it to my grandmother that the marriage of the century is off.'

His face remained impassive but he recognised that, whilst he would fast recover from the business of his broken engagement, it would be different for his grandmother. Depression was taking its toll. She refused to leave the house and travel to London, where he could keep a watchful eye on her, but she was distancing herself from her friends, going out less and less, and it worried him.

Gabriel's love for his independent and strong grandmother was his one weakness. She had never understood why he couldn't settle down.

'You work too hard.' She used to nag away at him as she bustled around, bringing him little delicacies she had cooked and treating him like the kid he no longer was. 'You need a wife, Gabriel, children—something to come home to at the end of the day.'

She would never understand that his father had had all that and had crumbled like a hollowed out shell the day it had been snatched away from him. She would never understand how Gabriel had watched from the sidelines and seen how love could destroy as much as it could nourish. His father had never recovered after his wife had died and that wasn't going to be Gabriel. He was never going to position himself in the firing line, open to hurt and devastation because he'd given his body and soul to someone else.

For him, marriage would be an arrangement, and he'd been happy to get engaged to Lucy and embark on just such an arrangement. He was thirty-four years old and the timing had been good. And, most importantly, it would have made his grandmother happy and, more than anything, Gabriel would have liked that.

His parents had died without the grandchildren they might have expected and he was determined that his grandmother wouldn't follow suit—he had a chance to provide great-grandchildren at least.

But love? No. He would happily leave that to other misguided souls.

'You were going to introduce her to Lucy, weren't you?'

'It's a shame. I think they would have got along.'

'What about the week we had planned there before that? Shall I cancel it?'

'Why would you do that?'

'Won't you want to spend some quality time with your grandmother on your own? I know you were staying with her while I went to the hotel, but won't work be a distraction you could do without?'

'And I thought you knew me,' Gabriel murmured.

'So we go as usual?'

'I will stay on after you've returned to London. That will please my grandmother.'

Abby thought that it might please her but it certainly wasn't going to make up for a broken engagement and saying goodbye to the pitter patter of little feet in due course.

All that normal stuff that happened to normal people.

For the first time, feelings carefully submerged burst their banks and came raging through. Memories of how her own heart had been broken, mangled and walked over, by an ex to whom she had been engaged. Memories of picking up pieces while facing the daily humiliation of carrying on in a tiny village where everyone knew everyone else and the story of her broken engagement had been headline news for months. She'd pinned a smile to her face for so long that her jaw had had a permanent ache from the strain of it. And her poor parents, so sympathetic, making sure to avoid talking about *that man* even though they still saw *that man's* parents all the time in the village. She and Jason had been childhood sweethearts before he'd been seduced first by London, then Paris and then a sexy little blonde who'd been thrilled to nab a hot shot banker.

She should have been turned off the whole business of love and marriage for good. Maybe the reason Jason had reared his ugly head out of the blue was because, faced with that very question, Abby had had to concede that there was still a part of her that longed for the fairy tale.

The normal stuff that happened to normal people, even if sometimes it ended up going wrong.

'Fine.' Her voice was clipped and she smiled blandly at Gabriel in a manner that suggested that, now that the message had been delivered, it was time for normality to return.

She'd had her heart broken but that had made her so much stronger.

'My perfect, efficient PA,' Gabriel murmured appreciatively. 'Time for work—and there's a lot to get through. Good to know that we're on the same wavelength—which is why I say that work goes on as normal when we go to Seville in a few days' time.'

CHAPTER TWO

'So…' SETTLED IN his seat, Gabriel finally turned his attention to his companion. 'I feel as though I haven't spoken to you for days'

'We had a long conversation yesterday about the two companies we're going to see outside Seville,' Abby pointed out. But he had a point. No sooner had he received the shocking news that his fiancée was no longer interested in the role than Gabriel had taken himself abroad for four days.

'Inconvenient,' he had told her in passing when she had showed up for work the day after her revelations about Lucy and Rupert. 'But that's what happens when you leave a boy to do a man's job. Reynolds has screwed up with the lawyers in New York and that deal looks as though it's going to be set back by two months if I don't get over there and iron things out.'

He'd emailed her the evening before, warning her of his forthcoming absence, but the office had still felt curiously empty once the door had slammed shut behind him. Needless to say, the list of things he wanted her to do was as long as her arm, but exhausted as she was at the end of each evening, she still managed to find time to speculate on his hurried departure from the office.

On the outside, Gabriel was the essence of charm. Physically beautiful, he knew just how to charm whatever he wanted from whoever happened to be withholding it from him—and, if that ploy failed, Abby had seen first-hand how fast that easy charm could give way to steely-eyed menace that left no one in any doubt that when it came to a fight he was prepared to go for it.

But underncath that charm, and underneath all that bluster about being fine with the break-up of his engagement, could Gabriel be hiding a vulnerable side?

Abby found herself wasting far too much time speculating about that. It was as if boundaries had suddenly been breached and now he'd somehow managed to stick his foot in the door and wedge open a part of her she had been keen to keep firmly closed.

Gabriel wasn't just like any other boss. There was just *too much* of him for comfort.

'What's our schedule going to be?' She pulled the conversation back into her safe comfort zone and slid calm, grey eyes over to him.

They were on his private jet. She'd been on this jet twicc and she knew that there was no relief from the intimacy of the surroundings. No hubbub of other passengers calling flight attendants for drinks, no announcements over the PA system reminding them of which countries they happened to be flying over, no distant wails of discontented toddlers. On the previous two occasions, there had at least been the distraction of several other employees who were being ferried over to work on the same deal but, even if there hadn't been, she wouldn't have approached the trip feeling as though she had to be careful.

And with good reason, judging from the amused look on Gabriel's face.

She hurriedly averted her eyes, only to be swamped by his suffocating masculine appeal as he sprawled in the leather seat, fingers loosely linked on his lap, his dark, spiky hair combed back so that there was nothing to distract from the angular, chiselled perfection of his lean features.

Gabriel could recognise a change of subject when he heard one and he was hearing one now. 'Well, I have to admit that things have changed slightly, thanks to Lucy's defection.'

He'd spoken to Lucy, and Abby had been accurate in her retelling of his ex-fiancée's reasons for returning the engagement ring to him.

'You're never around, Gabe,' she had said, looking at him with such apprehension that he'd had to force himself not to click his tongue with annoyance. Since when had he turned into an intimidating monster who ate innocent young girls for breakfast?

'I have a business to run,' he had explained. 'You've seen how that works. Your father is abroad a lot of the time.'

'And that's how I know that I don't want that for myself,' she had confided, her big, blue eyes wide. 'Dad was always away when I was growing up and I don't want that for my kids. I want them to have a Daddy who's there and not always on the other side of the world. Plus, what's the point of being married if you never get to see your husband? Gabe, we've been going out for seven months and I feel as though I have to book an appointment to see you.'

Since Gabriel couldn't argue with that, he'd maintained a tactful silence whilst she had gathered momentum and told him all the reasons why she had got cold feet, ending with a suitable apology and some hand wringing.

Lucy had wanted more than he had it in him to give. She had made him feel a hundred years old, jaded and cynical, but that was who he was, and he was never going to change. He'd hurried into something for all the right reasons, as far as he was concerned, but he'd failed to do his homework and now he could only wish her luck, when they parted company, with Rupert the chinless wonder who had, incredibly, become a male model.

'Your grandmother must have been disappointed,' Abby said sympathetically and Gabriel tilted his head to one side and shot her a rueful smile.

'I haven't broken the news to her just yet,' he admitted and Abby's mouth fell open.

'You haven't *told her*?'

'I thought it made more sense to do something like that face to face. Her health isn't great. The less time she has to brood over the great-grandchildren that won't be happening, the better.'

'So she still thinks that you're going over there on business and in a week's time Lucy will be joining you, the happy, radiant bride-to-be?'

'I never thought you could be so judgemental,' Gabriel said, unperturbed. He grinned. 'I'll be honest.' He leaned a little towards her and Abby automatically drew back. 'Ava refuses to go near a computer. I think the top-of-the-range one I bought her a year ago is currently rusting from lack of use, despite the fact that I spent half a day teaching her how to use it and left written instructions on sticky notes at the side. She also can't get her head around mobile phones and has yet to master text messaging. So, for practical reasons, face to face was always going to be the best method of delivery when it comes to the bad news.'

'She'll be shocked,' Abby murmured, thinking about how shocked her own parents had been when she'd told them the news about *her* broken engagement. 'Parents get their hopes up and then, when they're disappointed, it's almost worse for them than for…the child on the receiving end of the broken engagement.' Her eyes misted over and she blinked the memory away.

Addled, she stared down at her tablet and frantically tapped so that she could access the reports she had worked on, anything to focus Gabriel's attention on work, because she could feel those dark eyes of his boring into her.

'You're probably right,' Gabriel murmured. 'Parents do get their hopes up. And grandparents as well, of course.'

His shrewd eyes noted the way she was fiddling with the tablet. In a second she was going to shove something in front of him, a timely reminder to keep his distance. But something had changed between them and maybe, because he was a little unsettled by the business with Lucy, he couldn't help liking the frisson he felt in Abby's company. Maybe it was the element of distraction but she was occupying his mind in ways she hadn't done previously.

He was curious about her. He had to admit that it wasn't for the first time. When she'd first started working for him, he'd been curious about her, curious about that wall of permanent reserve she had around her, as though she'd erected a fortress complete with invisible 'no trespass' signs. Innocuous questions were met with bland replies and non-answers but, of course, she'd settled in and he'd quickly realised that he'd found himself the most efficient PA he could ever have hoped for. Given his chequered history when it came to PAs, he'd shelved all curiosity, because a good PA was worth her weight in gold and he wasn't about to jeopardise his good fortune by being nosy.

But now...

He looked at the sensible dark-grey trouser suit which screamed 'no nonsense'.

'Was that what you found?' he asked and Abby looked at him sharply.

'Sorry, but I'm not following you.'

Gabriel murmured piously, 'It's just that you seemed to be speaking from experience just then. When,' he elaborated to forestall any puzzled frowns, 'You said that parents and grandparents were often more upset by this sort of thing than the person actually going through it. So...were you speaking from experience?'

'Of course not,' Abby blustered, for once not her usual unflappable self. 'I just meant,' she added with a sudden urge to give him a taste of his own medicine, 'That your grandmother is going be so upset, when you say that she was looking forward to you settling down, and she'll be even more upset because you really don't seem that bothered at all.'

Gabriel grinned with open enjoyment which, Abby thought with some frustration, completely defeated the object of the exercise.

'Yet I'm sure she'll agree that it's better to have been ditched at the aisle than ditched post-vows.'

'I'm sure Lucy would have been a devoted wife if she'd married you.'

The smile faded from Gabriel's lips at the sincerity in her voice. 'Doubtless,' he drawled, half-closing his eyes and affording Abby a bird's eye view of his lush, dark lashes which would have been the envy of any woman. 'But, bearing in mind the disappointment she would have found at the end of the rainbow, I very much doubt her devotion would have been long lasting.'

'Why?' Abby heard herself ask. She was inviting just the sort of out-of-bounds conversation she had sworn to avoid but she couldn't seem to help herself.

Gabriel opened his eyes and looked at her lazily, his head tilted to one side as though he was debating the pros and cons of providing her with an answer to her question.

'Forget I asked,' Abby said stiffly. 'I'm not paid to ask personal questions.'

'Oh, for God's sake, Abby...'

'Well, I'm not!' Her mild grey eyes glinted.

'Do you avoid asking me questions because you don't want me to ask you any?'

'I avoid asking you questions, Gabriel, because, like I said, it's not part of my job remit.'

'Yet you probably know more about me than any other woman,' he mused. 'Maybe you know so much that you haven't got any questions to ask. After all, you have to admit that I'm an open book.'

'You're impossible.' She paused. 'And you're not an open book.'

'You've known every single woman I've ever dated since you started working for me,' Gabriel pointed out, enjoying the titillating undercurrent to their conversation, which he suspected she wished she'd never prolonged.

'I've hardly *known* them,' Abby said drily. 'Yes, I've made arrangements for the theatre, and restaurants and the opera, and, yes, a couple of them have come into the office at some point or other.'

'Not at my request.' Gabriel enjoyed a varied and plentiful love life but he'd always, with the exception of Lucy, disapproved of women dropping in to see him at the office. It was a level of familiarity on a par with doing a food shop together, cooking or watching television. Not to be encouraged.

'But you're far from being an open book,' she finished briskly. 'You're happy to be very transparent when it comes to some things but extremely opaque when it comes to others.'

Gabriel thought that she couldn't have summed him up more accurately if she'd tried, and for a few seconds he frowned, uncomfortable at that.

'Like I said,' he drawled, 'You know me better than anyone else.'

'That's because, through necessity, I spend an awful lot of time in your company.'

'Angling for a pay rise, Abby?'

Abby blushed. He was playing with her and she had to accept that she'd encouraged that by stepping into private territory which was normally out of bounds.

She also had to concede that when he spoke to her like that, his sexy voice deep, rich and velvety, a pleasurable tingle unfurled inside her. Yes, it was inappropriate, but it couldn't be helped.

No wonder women fell for the guy like ninepins. He

oozed easy charm, and when he turned it on thinking straight suddenly became very difficult.

'Far from it.' She located the reports waiting to be read and made a show of staring at them. If they hadn't been flickering on her tablet, she would busied herself rustling paper to get her point across. 'I'm not at all unhappy with my pay. Everyone in this business sector knows how generous you are when it comes to salaries.'

'No price too steep for loyalty,' Gabriel agreed. 'And in the world of technology, where secrets are begging to be shared with hungry competitors, loyalty is a valuable commodity. You're tapping your finger on your tablet. Is that your way of telling me that it's time we started talking about work?' He laughed softly and the hairs on the back of Abby's neck curled. 'Okay, off you go. I can tell you're dying to tell me what's in those reports of yours you're staring so hard at.'

Abby spun to look at him and breathed in deeply. In this mood, he unnerved her, made her forget the boundaries between them, and if she knew that she was partly to blame then that didn't matter. What mattered was the importance of the lines she had drawn between them from the very first day she'd started working for him.

It wasn't just because she knew the fate of the PAs who had preceded her, all shot down in flames for overstepping the line because. She'd gathered he'd always enjoyed having a pretty face around, and naturally, in the end, all those pretty faces had not been able to resist the lure of their sexy, charming boss. He had a special way of talking to you, a way that made you feel as though you were the only human being on earth he was interested in.

Abby had seen that in action when she'd been doing

something as harmless as reporting on a conversation she might have had about some deal or other, or suggestions she might have had about some of the programmes one of his many companies was developing—because he always encouraged suggestions, which was just one of the many ways he involved his employees and made them feel invaluable.

But now this...

This was different and it felt dangerous because he wasn't talking to her about work.

Abby had no intention of dropping her guard any more than she already had and, the sooner she filled him in on that, the better.

Because she'd always privately maintained that she was immune to his charm. She'd been jettisoned by a guy who'd been cute and charming and she knew better than to be taken in by someone like that again. Especially when she'd seen first-hand how many women were suckers for a man like Gabriel. She'd done far too much end-of-relationship flower-buying on his behalf, thank you very much!

But he was in a strange place, even if he wouldn't admit it, and it would seem, the devil was working on idle hands because that low-level teasing disturbed her. It was like having a feather brushed against her skin, giving her goose bumps, tickling her in places that made her blush.

Of course, he would return to normal soon enough, but just in case he decided that breaching the boundaries could become a permanent thing she felt that it was up to her to speak her mind.

She cleared her throat and looked him squarely in the eye.

'I feel uncomfortable saying this.' She hesitated, unsettled by his eyes which, now that she was staring into their depths, she noticed were the deepest and darkest of navy blue. 'But since we're going to be working with one another for the next week...'

'Nothing new there, Abby.'

'Yes, I know, but this is a little different. I realise I won't be staying with you in a hotel because you'll be at your grandmother's place, but we won't be in our... our...'

'Usual territory?' Gabriel inserted helpfully, intrigued by where this was leading.

'So things seem to have altered a little between us and I get that. I have never been involved in your private life before, not really, but I have been recently, through no fault of my own.' She glanced away because the intensity of his gaze was making her hot and bothered. She wished he'd say something but, perversely, he was silent, waiting for her to carry on or maybe, she thought, waiting for her to trip up with the tangled speech she'd begun without thinking through first.

'And for that I apologise,' Gabriel said seriously, eventually.

Their eyes met and there was a moment of perfect understanding between them. Beneath that grave tone, he was amused, and she knew it. She shot him a fulminating look of frustration and his lips twitched but he looked away, the thick fringe of his lashes concealing his expression.

'Apology accepted,' Abby said. 'But what I feel I must say is that I don't feel comfortable...er...er...'

Gabriel raised his eyebrows in an unspoken question and she gritted her teeth.

'I don't enjoy talking about my private life,' she finished lamely.

'I didn't think we were, Abby.'

'I have every sympathy for you, and I really feel for you having to break the news about Lucy to your grandmother, but I think we should move on and re-establish our...our...'

'Why are you so scared about opening up?' Gabriel asked softly and Abby was rattled enough to glare at him.

'That's exactly what I mean!' she cried. She was shocked when she slammed down the leather lid of her tablet.

Gabriel was fascinated. Somewhere, in the back of his mind, he'd registered that she was attractive enough but her whole face right now was alive with emotion. Her grey eyes had darkened, her full mouth was downturned in a pout of frustration and her cheeks were flushed.

Just like that, he wondered what she would look like naked. Naked on a bed, flushed from making love.

His mouth tightened and he shifted. 'Message received loud and clear, Abby,' he told her tightly. 'Strangely, what you call an infringement of your privacy, most normal people call good manners and polite curiosity. But, if you'd rather we stick exclusively to work-related issues, then that's fine with me.'

'Thank you,' she said tautly.

'I've already read all those reports you want to get through.'

'You have?'

'You emailed them to me yesterday.'

'And you've been in meetings most of the day.'

'It doesn't take me long to sift through the waffle and get to the bits that matter.' Without further ado, he began talking work. In depth. It was exactly what she had demanded, and she had no idea why she was suddenly disappointed that she'd put an end to their little foray into a less structured relationship.

Did she really want him asking her lots of personal questions? No! Did she want to be hostage to all sort of peculiar, inappropriate sensations because he happened to turn all that lazy male charm onto her? No! Because he was in an odd place didn't mean that he could entertain himself at her expense because there had been a temporary fissure in their usual rigid working relationship.

Once upon a time, when she'd been young, naïve and planning her happy-ever-after with Jason, she'd been open and trusting, but since then she'd erected more protective barriers than the Bank of England and she wasn't going to let them be demolished by her boss.

Abby didn't know why she felt the need to maintain all those barriers, because Gabriel had been right when he'd said that his questions weren't intrusive. They were just normal conversation between two people who happened to spend the majority of their waking hours together.

It was just that there was a quality of danger that clung to him. She'd sensed it as soon as she'd started working for him—an unpredictable charisma about him that could seduce the unwary, and it went far beyond the killer looks and the sharp intellect.

So she'd built her defence system even though she knew that he would never look at her twice anyway. She'd seen his girlfriends and they weren't average-looking women in their twenties with brown hair and grey eyes. They were voluptuous sex sirens, with the exception of Lucy, who had been so spectacularly pretty that when they were together it was almost a crime not to take a photo.

Abby surfaced to find him neatly concluding his monologue on the various legal loopholes they would have to look out for when they went to see his client the following day, and telling her to buckle up.

'I'll stop by my grandmother,' he explained as the jet began its descent, and Abby gazed out of the window, then turned to look at him.

'Fine.' She nodded. 'I have the address of the hotel. I'll get a cab there, shall I? And when we're not working I'm very happy to busy myself following up with the usual reports on what's been said so that you have everything to hand fairly immediately.'

'Very efficient,' Gabriel murmured. 'But I think it would be nice for you to meet Ava when we get there. When I disappear for hours on work-related business, she'll at least know who I'm with.'

'What else might she think you're doing?'

Gabriel dealt her a slashing smile. 'Who knows? She might think that a man with a broken heart might be looking for someone to help fix it.'

Abby reddened. Following on logically from that point, she could only conclude that, once Ava met her, her mind would be set at rest that her grandson was actually disappearing off to work because there was no way he could be doing anything else with someone like Abby.

She was in no doubt that he would certainly be looking for some sticking plaster in the form of his usual glamorous sex bombs just as soon as they returned to London.

'You must have spoken a great deal about Lucy,' Abby said conversationally, because they were landing and the silence was begging to be filled. Gabriel shot her a sideways glance.

'Virtually nothing,' he confessed. 'My grandmother disapproves of the women I tend to date.'

'She's met them?'

'One or two. The rest she's seen in various gossip columns. Her opinion seems to have stuck in a time warp roughly three years ago when I broke up with a glamour model who proceeded to do a kiss-and-tell story to one of the tabloids. I'm afraid she tarred and feathered the women who came after with the same brush as airheads willing to cash in on my name.'

Abby didn't say anything but she was on his grandmother's side, even though there had been no kiss-and-tell stories while she'd been working for him.

He stood up and Abby preceded him out of the plane, to be hit by a warm blast of air that momentarily took her breath away. 'So I thought that the less said, the better.'

He flushed darkly because the truth of the matter was he saw less of his grandmother than he should do, and spoke less to her than he ought to. It honestly hadn't occurred to him to launch into a lengthy touchy-feely conversation about Lucy, which wasn't his style anyway. And it was hardly as though the engagement had been a long-standing one. Four and a half weeks ago he had sat back in his chair in one of the top restaurants in central London and watched as she'd opened the box containing the diamond ring and gasped suitably.

She had slipped the six figures' worth of ring onto her finger, her eyes had grown teary and she had said, as it turned out with complete and utter honesty, that she'd had no idea...

Abby gave him a jaundiced look from under her lashes, and it hit him that she had to be the only woman in the world so openly sceptical of his motivations and so open about expressing it. She might give him long lectures about guidelines being kept and barriers not being breached, but she was kidding herself if she thought that those barriers weren't breached on a daily basis by that very way she had of looking at him, as she had just then.

'Did you send her pictures?' she asked, stepping into the long car waiting for them at the airfield. 'She surely must have been curious about the woman who was going to be your wife?'

'I've only been engaged for a month or so, Abby. Maybe I should have tasked you with the job of filling my grandmother in on all the details, bearing in mind I've been out of the country more than I care to think over the past few weeks.'

'I would never have done that!'

'No.' He shrugged. 'As it turns out, it's just as well that there were no photos sent. My grandmother knows about the engagement but that's about it. No details and, in fairness, her health has been poor, so she's not been as much on the ball as she usually would be.'

Abby looked at him narrowly and felt her pulses quicken as that illicit, forbidden thrill she'd felt earlier swooped through her in a rush. 'Are you saying that she has no idea who Lucy is at all?'

'Like I said,' Gabriel intoned silkily, 'I was hoping

for a pleasant surprise. I was going to do the introduction with a flourish.' He looked through the window, frowning. 'Just as well, in a way, that she never met Lucy, didn't even know her name and certainly didn't ask for photos so that she could start picturing what the great-grandchildren would look like.'

He sighed and Abby looked at him, seeing the crack in his self-assurance. He'd said practically nothing to the woman who meant so much to him, She wondered whether, subconsciously, he had been as hesitant about Lucy as Lucy had been about him, in the end. Had he ticked all the right boxes, yet known that no amount of ticking could take the place of love and what it brought to a union?

'I'm sure she'll take it on the chin.' Abby resorted to cheerful optimism and Gabriel turned to her with a grin.

'We'll find out soon enough. I, personally, have always found that it's easy to accept what you can't change.'

Their eyes tangled and she couldn't tear her gaze away. She felt suddenly lost, drowning in the deep, dark depths, and when she did manage to look away her nerves were all over the place and she had to inhale deeply, sucking the air in like a drowning man gasping for oxygen.

They were soon in the town and she was relieved when he began talking to her about the city. Her nerves calmed. They had left behind the cool, grey skies of London and the dense, crowded pavements. Here, the sky was milky blue and the sun was bright but with the pleasant coolness of a fine spring day. There were people everywhere as the sleek, black car navigated the picturesque roads of the town but no sense of claustrophobia. The buildings were beautiful, faded sepia and yellow, the architecture graceful. It was a town that was conducive to meandering.

'Will your driver wait to take me to the hotel?' she asked when he informed her that they would be at his grandmother's house in under fifteen minutes.

'He'll do what I tell him to,' Gabriel responded with the sort of casual arrogance that she found annoying and weirdly endearing in equal measure. A short while later, he announced, 'And here we are.'

The city had been left behind, replaced by tall trees and a cool, forested area speckled with houses, each standing in its own grounds.

'The residents here enjoy their privacy,' Gabriel said with satisfaction. 'And they've been prepared to pay for it. It's designed with interesting short cuts between the properties so that the neighbours can visit one another, and there's a golf course surrounding the entire compound like a bracelet. All in all, this has been a great investment.'

'It belongs to *you*?'

'Are you impressed?'

'I thought you concentrated on buying and selling companies and in technology and communication,' she said frankly.

'I'm a man of varied interests,' he said smoothly, in response. 'There's nothing I won't try my hand at.' With rare introspection he wondered if that was why he had guiltily plunged into an ill-fated engagement to please his grandmother and was now facing the prospect of letting her down without warning.

Because he would try his hand at anything in business, the riskier the venture the better, but that was where his thirst for adventure stopped. Maybe now it was time to admit to his grandmother that he was never going to give her the fairy story she'd always wanted for him.

CHAPTER THREE

ABBY DIDN'T KNOW what to expect when the car finally pulled up in front of a low, sprawling villa with a plantation-style feel. Shallow steps led up to a wide veranda, on which was an arrangement of chairs and tables. On either side of the house, manicured lawns gave way to thick, colourful foliage and sweeping trees that cast shadows over the courtyard.

Gabriel's hand was poised to ring the doorbell when the door was pulled open, and he looked down at his grandmother who was in her Sunday best and had obviously been glued to the window, waiting for his arrival.

Behind him, he knew that Abby was hovering.

Gabriel knew that he should have tackled the business of his broken engagement earlier, flown over as soon as he'd known that there was not going to be a wedding, sat down and explained it to her. She was thinner than he remembered, and she was smiling broadly, tugging him inside, but there was a frailty about her that was a little alarming.

How was she going to take what he had to say?

He'd been in weekly contact with her doctor, although she was unaware of that, and he knew that stress was something she had to avoid.

'And depression,' her consultant had said to him. Gabriel had never known his grandmother to be depressed but now he wasn't so sure.

'Here at last!' Ava was doing her best to peer round her grandson. 'I've been counting down, *nipote caro*.'

'I have been busy.' Gabriel immediately launched into a guilty apology. 'My feet have barely touched the ground in the past couple of months…'

'Well, I'm sure that young lady of yours is going to do something about that,' Ava chided, finally circling Gabriel and inquisitively looking at Abby, who had not followed her boss in but was sticking close to the courtyard because she didn't foresee a protracted visit. 'Won't you, *mio caro*?'

Abby's mouth opened. Ava was tiny, her dark eyes bright and curious, her grey hair cut into a short, sharp bob which should have made her seem severe, but didn't, because she had a face that was creased with laughter lines. She had greeted Gabriel in Italian but now switched to English, which was heavily accented but excellent.

'Are you going to do the introductions?' Ava half-turned to Gabriel, who towered over her. 'I've never known you to be rude, Gabriel!'

'Abby.' Gabriel obliged, half-occupied with something on his phone so that he glanced up but briefly. 'This is Ava, my indomitable grandmother, who runs rings round me every time I come here to visit.'

'Which isn't nearly often enough.' Ava reached to take Abby's hand, tugging her into the hallway. 'Even as a little boy,' she confided, leading the way into the house as Abby cast a backward glance at the sleek car which should have been driving her to her hotel. The driver was standing in the sun, leaning against the car, scrolling through his phone.

'He was always in a hurry.'

'Who? Sorry, what?' The front door had closed. Abby met Gabriel's eyes over Ava's head and recognised instantly that there would be little assistance coming from that direction because he was still frowning at his phone—which was downright *rude*, all things considered.

'Gabriel, dear. I expect you know my husband and I brought him up after his parents, God rest their souls, died prematurely. It was never a burden. He was a joy.'

'He's hardly a joy now,' Abby was tempted to say with a rebellious streak of wickedness. 'Picking up a phone call when he has *so much* he wants to say to you.'

Gabriel grinned and raised his eyebrows. 'You sound like a wife,' he drawled. 'And a shrewish one at that.'

Ava clapped her hands and burst out laughing, delighted at this exchange because, Abby thought, huffing at the amused glint in Gabriel's eyes, she was unaware of the undercurrent.

Gabriel picked up where he had left off, moving to lean into her, his mouth close to her ear, which made her shiver and go hot. 'Maybe that's what happens when two people spend so much time together. Think that's it?'

'I'm tired,' Abby whispered back pointedly. 'Isn't it about time I get to the hotel? You can email me whatever work you want me to do tonight.'

'No rush.' Gabriel's deep, dark eyes met hers and Abby thought with a little frisson of panic that the quicker she got to her hotel, the better. But Ava was leading the way into a sitting room and a maid had appeared from nowhere with a tray of little nibbles and an ornate silver pot of coffee.

'I have a selection of teas as well.' Ava patted a sofa and Abby somehow found herself sinking into it. 'And cold drinks. Or would you be happy with coffee?'

Abby smiled at the small woman, thawing at her warmth. When Jason had betrayed her, she had developed a tough outer shell to cope with the pieces she had been left picking up. She'd had to deal with pitying neighbours and over-sympathetic friends and then, having moved to London to begin life without the security of an engagement ring on her finger, she had toughened up even more.

She had almost forgotten the young girl who had laughed easily, but something about his grandmother put her at her ease. She couldn't have been more different from her grandson.

'Coffee's fine.' Abby glanced around her. Out of the corner of her eye, she noted that Gabriel was having an urgent discussion with someone on his phone and she stifled a sigh of impatience. 'You have a wonderful house—so lovely and airy—it must be a joy to live here.'

'It's far too big, dear...' Ava sighed and looked at Gabriel.

'He only ever thinks about work.' Abby found herself excusing him.

On cue, Gabriel proved her point by breaking off his phone call to inform them that he had to take the call. 'You know what my life's like, Abby,' he said, sucking her in to support him. 'She keeps me in check, Grandma, but sometimes needs must.'

He left the room, quietly shutting the door behind

him, and Abby prepared herself for the long haul because, from experience, Gabriel could spend an hour on the phone if it was urgent enough and he rarely seemed to mind who was left twiddling their thumbs and biding their time.

'He's very lucky to have found you,' Ava said, sipping coffee and shooting Abby a speculative look that was very much like her grandson's. 'Every man, even that powerhouse grandson of mine, needs to be kept in check. I don't suppose he's told you about some of the things he got up to when he was a child?' Ava didn't wait for a response, which was just as well, because Abby would have been tempted to tell her that those sorts of personal conversations didn't appear on their daily radar.

'Well.' Ava reached under the coffee table in front of them and pulled out a photo album, which touched Abby, because it was clear that the elderly woman was fond of looking back through old photos. 'Let me show you some pictures of when Gabriel was a young boy,' she said, flipping through the enormous album with familiarity. 'I don't suppose he has any of these lying around? No, I didn't think so. Boys can be so unsentimental. I would have loved to have had a granddaughter but it wasn't to be. Still, we mustn't complain about cards we have been dealt, must we?'

Abby thought of her crap hand with Jason and laughed in agreement. Curiosity fully roused, she settled into looking at pictures of Gabriel, lovingly taken over the years.

He had been so breathtakingly good-looking from an early age that she found herself absently tracing some of the images with her finger as she sipped her coffee.

It was little wonder he was so confident when it came to the opposite sex, she thought. Pictures of him as a teenager showed a tall, strikingly beautiful young man, conscious of the lens directed at him but careless about posing for it.

She was hardly aware of Gabriel entering the room until he said, leaning over them both, 'Enjoying yourself?'

Abby sat back and yanked her wandering fingers away from the pages of the album.

'Phone call finished?' she asked sweetly. 'Because, if it is, then perhaps I could...' She smiled at Ava and began rising to her feet. 'Thank you so much for showing me that album.' She slid a sly sideways glance at Gabriel. 'I'll remember those pictures for as long as I live. It's always a revelation to see photos of people as children, especially when you can't really picture those people as ever being young.'

Gabriel was smiling but there was something in his eyes that made Abby pause for a few seconds.

Ava turned to her grandson with a severe expression. 'Why isn't there an engagement ring?'

'Sorry?' Abby was smiling. Gabriel was frowning. And both of them were staring at the diminutive figure on the sofa with varying degrees of bewilderment.

'You're not wearing an engagement ring, dear.' Ava clicked her tongue and gave Gabriel a roguish grin that made her seem years younger and made Abby think that, as a young woman, she would have been truly beautiful. 'It's probably something young people do nowadays. Goodness only knows, it's none of my business—because the main thing is that you love one another and you're going to be married—but it would have been unthinkable in my day for a young lady who was engaged not to have an engagement ring on her finger!'

Ava chuckled into the stunned silence that greeted this remark. 'Unless you've been thinking of your mother's engagement ring, Gabriel?' Ava sighed. 'You probably haven't been. You're not given to gestures like that, but I know Alicia would have been so happy. But please forget I said anything!' She waved one hand sheepishly while the silence pooled, gathered and collected until Gabriel broke it to murmur warmly.

'You've never shown me my mother's personal belongings.'

Ava's eyes lit up and a she fairly leapt to her feet. 'I never thought you were interested and I didn't like to push anything.' She began walking slowly to the door but not until she had patted Abby on the hand. 'I'm so happy,' she whispered. 'You've made an old lady so happy.'

The door shut and for a few seconds Abby's mind was a complete blank. Her mouth was open, and she dimly thought that she probably resembled a fish, gasping for water because somehow it had managed to find itself stranded on dry land. Maybe a motorway. Somewhere very far from water. Then she shot to her feet and stood right in front of Gabriel, hands on her hips.

'What the heck is going on?'

'Drink?' He led the way out of the living room, pausing only to tell Ava, who was still shuffling off towards the side of the house, that she could take her time because there were one or two things he needed to chat to Abby about.

'I'll be for ever.' Ava chuckled, while Abby wildly tried to shuffle her brain into doing something useful. 'There's a lot of stuff to rifle through. I'm a hoarder,

my dear. For my sins. You two make yourself at home!
I'll come down to the kitchen just as soon as I have
found the ring and other bits of jewellery. Such beautiful things. It'll be wonderful seeing them worn again.
It has been such a long time coming.'

'Drink?' Gabriel repeated, closing the kitchen door
behind him. 'Wine? Prosecco? Something with more
of a kick?'

Abby looked at him without really focussing. She
registered in some part of her brain that they were in
the most enormous kitchen she had ever been in. It was
dominated by an island, on which was a vase of wildly
beautiful flowers that filled the room with a sweet fra-
grance that made her head hurt.

She wobbled her way over to the eight-seat rectan-
gular table, which looked as old and weathered as the
beautifully mismatched chairs around it, and plonked
herself down while Gabriel poured them both a glass
of wine.

'You're shocked,' he said gravely, pulling a chair
close to her so that he didn't have to raise his voice.

'Well-detected, Sherlock Holmes.' Abby abandoned
all pretence of being the detached, professional, self-
composed PA she had spent the past two years culti-
vating.

She looked at him and took a healthy gulp of wine,
grimacing for a few seconds, then following it up with
another, more restrained sip.

'Your grandmother thinks… She thinks that somehow… Why didn't you *say something*?'

'I didn't have a great deal of time to plan ahead.'

'What does *planning ahead* have to do with anything?' Abby cried. 'Your grandmother has somehow

got hold of the wrong end of the stick, and now she's dashed off upstairs to find your *mother's ring* so that you can stick it on *my finger* because suddenly I've turned into your *fiancée*!'

'I was on the phone to her consultant.'

'What?'

'The important call I had to take. It wasn't work-related, as it happens. I'd made an appointment to see my grandmother's consultant as soon as I got to Seville. It should have been a face-to-face meeting, but unfortunately he's had to fly to Madrid because his grandson has been rushed to hospital with a medical emergency.'

'What does this have to do with anything?' Abby wondered whether she'd actually gone mad and was now inhabiting a parallel universe where normal rules no longer applied.

'He had something rather sensitive to talk about, hence his insistence that we meet, but failing that he felt he should let me know that, a few months ago, my grandmother had to be rushed into hospital with a suspected overdose.'

'What?'

'She insisted at the time that she got confused and took more of her medication than intended but her doctor, whilst ninety percent sure that she was telling the truth, felt that he was obliged to let me know that she was on tablets for depression at the time, so there was a chance that she had, indeed, tried to overdose.'

'My goodness!'

'My grandmother is extremely proud and she would loathe me knowing this but, unfortunately, it has some bearing on what's happening now.'

'Why don't I like the sound of this?'

'Have another swig of wine, or would you rather something a bit stronger?'

'Do I need something stronger? Brandy? Whisky? A slug of methylated spirits?'

'Why have you spent two years keeping your sense of humour hidden away?'

Abby blushed and glared at him, and he held his hands up in mock surrender.

'I knew nothing of my grandmother's depression, and for that I blame myself. I took my eye off the ball and then thought I could make it right by doing what she's wanted me to do for a long time—getting engaged. Finding someone willing to put up with me, dragging her kicking and screaming up the aisle and then proceeding to have a series of mini mes.'

'This isn't funny, Gabriel.' But she knew that he was keeping it light because it was less alarming that being utterly and deadly serious.

'When I told her that I was going to be married, when I made arrangements to visit her here with my fiancée, she immediately went to the consultant and handed over the rest of the anti-depressants. Said she didn't need them any more because she had something to live for.'

'Oh, Gabriel. What on earth are you going to do?'

'She's rushed into thinking that you're my fiancée.'

'Yes,' Abby said simply. For one, brief, treacherous moment she wondered what it would be like to be that woman, the woman with Gabriel's ring on her finger. A leggy, well connected Lucy-like stunner who would go on to have loads of little Gabriels....

'I can't really believe it,' she murmured with complete honesty.

'Can't believe what? She had no idea what Lucy

looked like, didn't even know her name. It happened very fast and, like I said, I'd hoped for the big surprise. When you think about it, it's little wonder she's jumped to the wrong conclusion. I may have mentioned in passing that I would be doing some work while I was over here. I can't remember if I said anything about bringing my PA.'

He paused thoughtfully, sipped his wine, looked at Abby's flushed face and admired the fact that, while she was obviously host to a certain amount of panic and bewilderment, she was still managing to keep her head and not give in to hysterics. He liked that. Always had.

'My grandmother gets confused.' He felt a tightness in his chest when he said that because he had vivid memories of what life had been like growing up under her loving tutelage. Where had the time gone? She'd once been as sprightly as a cricket. She and his grandfather had done everything for him. Had she started going downhill when his grandfather had died?

He had seen how much his father had suffered after his own mother had died, after which they had both gone to live with his grandparents. Gabriel had been very young, though. Had he been so absorbed learning his own life lessons at that point that he had switched off his emotions completely? Shut down his ability to empathise just in case he got caught up in a tangle of emotions that might drag him under, as they had his own father?

He'd been sworn off love but had he been sworn off everything else?

Had he quietly closed himself off so that he had become a spectator?

He loathed this self-pitying train of thought and he scowled and shifted in the chair.

'I don't mean *that*,' Abby said impatiently. 'I mean it's ludicrous that your grandmother would even think that someone like me could end up being engaged to someone like you!' She laughed a little self-consciously but when she met his gaze it was to find that he didn't share the joke.

'What do you mean?'

'C-come off it, Gabriel,' Abby stammered, feeling her way forward and wishing she hadn't opened her big mouth and said anything, but the words had just come out of her unfiltered.

'Explain. I'm not following you.'

'You said yourself that you got engaged to Lucy because she ticked all the right boxes: well connected, beautiful, the sort of person who would easily fit into your social circle...'

'I seem to have been remarkably descriptive on the subject,' Gabriel murmured, absorbed by the shifting patterns of discomfort and embarrassment on her face.

'I'm nothing like Lucy.' She laughed in a halting fashion. 'So I'm just surprised that Ava would have jumped to the wrong conclusion so easily. She must know that you're attracted to beautiful women.'

'I never thought you were self-conscious about your looks.'

'I'm not!' But her face was beetroot-red, and burning as though she'd gone up in flames. She wanted to say something glib and humorous to change the subject. She would even have settled for something prissy and stern, both mood-killers, but her tongue was glued to the roof of her mouth and her vocal cords had completely dried up.

'Good,' Gabriel said softly, 'Because you shouldn't

be.' He touched the side of her face, but only for a few seconds, and just like that Abby's breath hitched in her throat and she was painfully aware of her body in ways that were appalling and unimaginable.

Her nipples stiffened and her breasts were suddenly heavy and tender, weighing like ripe fruit against the lacy cotton of her bra. Those uninvited ripples of sensual awareness were unexpected and alarming.

He'd whipped his hand away, but where he had touched her stung, and she had to resist the urge to cool it with the palm of her hand. She didn't want to do that because she had no idea what sort of message that would convey and she wasn't going to take the chance.

'I'm going to ask something very big of you, Abby, and there's not going to be a whole lot of time to think about it.'

'No.'

'I haven't asked yet.'

'You don't have to—and, no, I won't pretend to be your fiancée because your grandmother's made a simple mistake. You need to be honest with her and tell her the truth.' She thought of the way the elderly woman's eyes had lit up at the mention of her daughter's jewellery and then chased that thought away in case it undermined her determination.

Gabriel vaulted to his feet and paced the kitchen, as restless as a bear confined in a cage.

He didn't look at her—seemed barely aware of his surroundings. Eventually, though, he stood in front of her and said roughly, with deadly seriousness, 'She's a lot more fragile than I ever imagined. I haven't been here for her.'

He looked away and raked his fingers through his

dark hair. 'I got lost in my work and allowed things to slip.' He made an all-encompassing gesture with his hand. 'When I bought her this, after my grandfather died, I did it to clear my conscience. These are things I have never discussed with anyone,' he continued with none of his usual grace and Abby felt as though she was glimpsing the real man behind the sexy, charming guy she worked for.

This was Gabriel, the essence of him, a man who kept his emotions under tight control until, now, he couldn't. Her heart went out to him and something seemed to slip a little under her feet. It was as if she'd been walking on solid ground only to discover that it wasn't as solid as she'd thought.

'Gabriel,' she protested helplessly.

'I fear for her,' he said quietly. 'After what her doctor has confided, it would seem that there is a great deal going on under the surface. She's found a new lease of life. You heard her. I fear for what might happen if that lease of life is taken away from her, which it would be, should she find out that there's no engagement.'

'Parents get over these disappointments.'

'Like yours did? Is that what happened, Abby? Did some guy put a ring on your finger and then break your heart by taking it away?'

Abby swallowed hard and looked away. She stared through the window at the velvety night outside, so different from the darkness of London, where it was really never that dark because of the street lamps.

'We're not talking about me,' she said gruffly.

'Do this for me and you can name your price,' Gabriel said flatly and her head snapped up.

'That's not how I operate, Gabriel!'

He remained silent until she sighed, scarcely believing that she was having this conversation. 'You can't buy me. I know you feel that money can get you anything you want, but it can't.'

In the past two weeks, it felt as though a house of cards had come tumbling down. In a heartbeat, Abby the efficient, contained professional had opened a door and a rush of wind had entered, bringing with it a tumult of emotions. 'Even if I agreed to this, lying can never be condoned, and what happens when the truth comes out? Ava will be so deeply hurt that you led her on and that I did too.'

'Why would she find out?'

'What do you mean?'

'Don't think of it as a *lie*,' Gabriel urged, leaning forward and letting his hands drop between his legs. 'Think of it as a simple charade, with an end in sight and a goal in mind.'

'That's just a clever play with words, Gabriel.' She shot him a wry look from under lashes and he had the grace to flush.

'We maintain a pretence while we're over here. In the meantime, I will try to find out what her depression is about, try and...' he paused and shook his head '... make up for the time I should have spent visiting and sitting down with her, instead of phoning on the hop between business deals in different countries.'

Abby didn't say anything. Her breathing was shallow and she glanced away for a few seconds.

'And then? What happens next in this scenario?'

'We return to London and inevitably we break up. These things happen but, by that point, I will have at least gone some way to repairing the fissure in our relationship. I might even,' he mused thoughtfully, 'Try and persuade her to semi-emigrate to London, or perhaps to one of those leafy suburbs outside London. She loves living here, so it's a long shot, but I would be far more accessible if we were to live in the same country.' He looked at Abby. 'In fact, you could start investigating that.'

'Investigating what?'

'Houses in leafy suburbs within commuting distance of London. Have a short list drawn up. Money no object.'

'Gabriel, that's not how things work.'

'Of course it is. I'm sure I'll be able to persuade my grandmother on the advantages of moving and, once she's close by and our convenient charade is at an end, I can put my mind to actually finding a woman more suitable to my needs than Lucy was.'

Abby's stomach tightened. Did he have any idea how insulting that remark was? No, of course he didn't, because although he might pat her hand and tell her to buck up because she wasn't the back end of the bus she'd made herself out to be, it was farcical to think that they could ever be a couple.

She was mortified that she had gone a little fuzzy round the edges when he had looked at her with those brooding dark eyes and told her that she shouldn't run herself down in the looks department.

'What a nuisance for you that Lucy didn't end up ticking all the right boxes,' she said coolly. 'Now you'll have to go through the process all over again. Question, however—don't you think your grandmother might see that, in your rush to the altar, you're not actually in love with the woman with the ring on her finger?'

Gabriel laughed and sat back. 'No, not really, now that you mention it. She wants me to be happy and she will see that I'm happy. Straightforward.'

'And the love element won't matter.'

'Love doesn't equate to happiness for everyone, Abby. Now, shall we wrap up this intense conversation and get back to the matter in hand? You want nothing from me. You're insulted that I would dare ask you to name your price for doing something that will undoubtedly benefit an old woman whose health is compromised. So, Abby, will you do this for me simply because I'm asking you to—as nothing more than a favour?'

His voice was soft and low and made her feel giddy and girlish.

'I won't do it for you, Gabriel, but I *will* agree to this for your grandmother's sake. I understand what you're saying about her health. My mother hasn't been great over the past six months. In fact, she's had shingles, and on the back of that her health has taken a knocking and she's ended up in hospital with pneumonia. It's been desperately worrying and she's been under medical advice to take things easy. My dad and I have likewise been warned about the damage that can be caused by stress.'

She paused and blinked furiously then took a deep breath and looked at him steadily. 'My dad's cashed in all his shares and used up his pension so that he can take Mum on a round-the-world cruise, so I understand that there are no limits when it comes to doing what it takes for someone you care about.'

Gabriel looked at her pensively. That level of devotion was just the thing that had made him cynical. He had been much younger, of course, and more impressionable, but he had seen what happened when one half of a partnership like that died: utter devastation. A parent in mourning with no time or energy left for the living, for a child who might need parental support all the more, only to find it missing in action.

On top of that, Abby had obviously gone through some sort of ordeal with a man.

And yet here she was, talking about love as though it was something to be lauded instead of avoided at all costs.

Could he trust her not to read more into a one-week charade than was actually there? he wondered.

Two weeks ago, he would have bet his penthouse apartment that his efficient, prim and remote PA was as cool in the emotional stakes as he was, yet he was getting to know more and more about her, and his views were changing fast.

She might be ice on the outside but the inside was a different matter altogether...

She knew him, of course, knew the sort of women he was attracted to, and even knew what he was looking for in a marriage. Did he have to spell anything out?

'My grandmother will be down shortly,' he said. 'And, whilst I am deeply grateful for your offer to...help me out in this matter, now that I think about it, I would rather keep things on a business footing. It would probably be for the best.' He smiled crookedly and said, with absolute sincerity, 'A practical arrangement is something I would feel at home with and, bearing that in mind, I have a proposition I think you'd like...'

CHAPTER FOUR

KEEP IT STRICTLY BUSINESS, Gabriel thought. With signatures on the dotted line, there would be no room for unfortunate misunderstandings. Favours had a nasty habit of backfiring and, in this instance, any backfiring could get…complicated. He wanted no emotional entanglements. No ghostly, shadowy *possibility* of any emotional entanglements.

That was something he would take away from the Lucy episode. He had foolishly thought that all cards had been put on the table. He'd never mentioned love, had never whispered sweet nothings. He had presented her with marriage as a union between two people who got along. How he had ever come to that conclusion baffled him in retrospect because Lucy, nice as she was, had been far too refreshingly naïve for his jaded soul.

But he'd been seduced by the allure of making his grandmother happy, accepting the fact that he really wasn't interested in remaining single for ever, and had been abroad for so much of their extremely brief courtship that he had had no opportunity really to discover the cracks until they'd opened up into an unbreachable chasm.

If he'd been more businesslike from the beginning

things would never have progressed to the point where Lucy had ended up hurt and bewildered, something for which he took full blame. She would have tossed him out on his ear without him coming to the end of his proposal!

Instead, he had made sweeping and egotistical assumptions that the bottomless vastness of his bank balance would be sufficient pull for any woman to adhere to what he wanted.

Next time round—and there would be a next time round—he would find a woman as career-driven as he was for whom marriage would be a mutually acceptable union between two people for whom work would always hold centre stage.

An independent woman, wealthy in her own right, who wasn't hankering to be swept off her feet and fed nonsense about happy endings.

It would be a challenge finding such a woman but since when did he ever shy away from a challenge? And, once his grandmother accepted that he was sincere and serious about finding a life partner more suitable than the women he had dated in the past, she would be happy and would easily move past the small matter of his so-called broken engagement to Abby.

In the meantime, this charade was essential. He would never be able to live with himself if the single most important person in his life were to slide into irreversible depression because of him. And the charade would only be possible because of Abby.

Which didn't mean that he was going to trust her to stick to the guidelines.

Not everyone was as strong-minded as he was. He knew himself and knew exactly what he was capable of. It was a strength that would ensure he would never be vulnerable, and he liked that.

'Let me go and check on my grandmother,' he said, standing up and stretching, flexing his muscles. 'She's probably got lost in reminiscing over old photos while hunting down my mother's jewellery. I'll make sure she's okay and then we can finish this conversation outside.'

Abby watched, unwillingly fascinated at the latent strength of his lean, muscular body. She lowered her eyes and nodded. 'Shall I meet you out…er…there?'

'There is seating on the veranda overlooking the gardens at the back. If you use that door—' he nodded to the kitchen door '—you just need to circle to the left, directly facing the swimming pool. I'll see you there in ten. And, Abby…grab yourself another drink or anything else you want from the fridge.'

'Think I might need sustenance for the conversation ahead of me?' she quipped and Gabriel grinned, that slow, amused, unconsciously wildly sexy grin that made all her bones turn to water, something she had managed quite successfully to fend off for two years but which she was finding impossible to ignore now.

He'd always admired her understated intelligence but he was seeing that, unleashed, her dry sense of humour was strangely similar to his own, which doubtless was why he was enjoying it so much.

'A stiff drink is always a handy prop in stormy seas…'

'Why are the seas going to be stormy, Gabriel?'

'Hopefully they won't be. I think you'll find my proposition very interesting, just so long as you don't allow your pride to stand in the way of accepting it.

Now, let me go and find my grandmother. I don't want to…open negotiations with my eye on the clock in case she returns. I'll make sure she's settled, and she can join us in due course. And, while I'm gone, you can think about the pride standing in the way of the situation.'

Abby opened her mouth to dispute that but remained silent because, yes, she was proud. She was just surprised that it was a trait he had managed to pick up on but then, as he had pointed out earlier, when you worked alongside someone as closely as they had worked together it was impossible not to pick up all sorts of things along the way.

That thought suddenly and inexplicably made the hairs on the back of her neck stand on end and she licked her dry lips.

'I'll…er…help myself to a glass of water, if that's all right.' She followed suit and stood up to discover that, instead of politely stepping away, Gabriel remained just where he was so that they were suddenly very close to one another, her breasts almost touching his chest.

Instinctively she stumbled back, bumping into the chair behind her so that he reached out to steady her.

'Are you already swept off your feet at the prospect of being my wife?' He loosed a low, amused laugh which irritated Abby, because she knew that underneath the silky, light banter there was a thread of sarcasm there that bordered on being insulting.

She was conscious of her formal clothing, appropriate for work and certainly not for a romantic tryst in a foreign city with a fiancé. How on earth had his grandmother not picked up on that? If she had met any of Gabriel's past girlfriends, then surely she would have thought it odd that the woman he was suddenly engaged to hadn't shown up wearing next to nothing so that she could display endless legs and cleavage?

'Sadly for your ego, Gabriel, no, I'm not. You have nothing to fear in that area.' She brushed his arm away and straightened herself, smoothing her skirt and her hair and then folding her arms. 'I have my head firmly screwed on.' She reverted to type as a reminder to him that she was far from the sort of ditzy girl who would let a one-week game of pretence go to her head.

'Splendid! And as my highly efficient secretary whose head is always firmly screwed on, consider job number one of this assignment to be cancelling your hotel room. I can't think of any reason why we should hang onto it, do you? It would be highly irregular for my fiancée to set up camp on the other side of the city...'

He grinned and moved to the kitchen door. 'Even my grandmother, old-fashioned as she is, would find that a bit peculiar. Cancel the room, and if they give you any trouble you can smooth the waters by reserving their conference room for our meetings. I had planned on paying on-site visits to the prospective clients but, given the change in circumstances, I think the less time we're on the road the better. I'll get the clients to do the running.'

'Of course.' She smiled and half-turned, and was relieved when she heard the quiet click of the kitchen door behind him as he went in search of his grandmother.

It gave her time to think about what had happened in the space of a handful of hours.

Like a puppet whose strings have been abruptly cut, she hobbled back to the table and sat, as weak as a kitten.

How had the lines between them become blurred so fast? Yes, of course she knew—he could work *that* out logically enough—but it was more than a simple case of lines being blurred.

Something had shifted dramatically and it terrified her. She didn't want Gabriel changing the goal posts. He had the sort of personality that was big enough to suffocate her and she was only realising now how many defence mechanisms she had put into place to combat the threat.

Conscious of her past experience with Jason, all too aware that her own soft nature and desire to be loved and to trust had been her undoing, she had assumed the tough outer shell she had erected around herself to be weatherproof.

Her brilliant, powerful and unpredictable boss, she'd told herself from their very first moment of meeting, was just the sort she could never be attracted to and that had become a valuable mantra over time.

After Jason, she was no longer in the market for anyone charming or good-looking. If he had the slightest whiff of unreliability about him, then he could be safely consigned to the incinerator.

Gabriel, she had seen first-hand, had managed to turn unreliability into an art form. When it came to women, he had the attention span of a toddler in a candy shop. She'd told herself that she almost didn't have to be careful around him because he was just so inappropriate for her!

Frankly, she felt sorry for the women he went out with. Hadn't they suspected from the get-go that he was as unreliable as they got?

But here she was now: blurred lines. Thoughts all over the place. Rollercoaster emotions doing all sorts of weird somersaults and back flips.

All hot and bothered, she went outside, easily locating the seating area he had told her about.

Glassy-eyed, she sat and stared out at a picture-perfect landscaped setting.

If Gabriel's intention had been to locate his grandmother in the most peaceful setting possible that was still close to the amenities of a city, then he couldn't have been more successful. It was hard to believe that somewhere as vital and bustling as Seville was only a matter of a drive away, because it was as quiet here as the deepest countryside, with an uninterrupted vista of green.

She stilled at the sound of footsteps but only looked at Gabriel when he had pulled up a chair to sit next to her, a refilled glass of wine in hand.

He wasn't looking at her as he delved into his pocket and withdrew a box, which he slid over to her.

Abby opened it and swallowed. 'I can't.' She snapped the box shut.

'Not to your taste?' Gabriel drawled.

'You know that's not it,' Abby intoned, relieved that they weren't face to face but instead both staring forward, out toward the dark shadow of the pool bordered with shrubs, trees and manicured lawns, liberally interrupted with flower beds, then, beyond that, to the necklace of rolling green fairways that circled the compound.

It was easier to talk when his dark, unsettling eyes weren't pinned to her face, depriving her of breath.

'Don't worry, it isn't a declaration of intent, and you don't get to keep it.'

'I know *that*,' Abby said sharply. 'I'm not a complete idiot, Gabriel. Like I said, you don't have to worry that I might start thinking that this charade is for real.'

'Sure about that?' Gabriel's voice was light, but there was an underlying seriousness beneath the casual tone that made her teeth snap together.

There was so much she wanted to tell him and she fought to remember that he was her boss and that, when this was over, she didn't want to have said anything she might later come to regret.

'Quite sure,' she confined herself to telling him, and he chuckled.

'My grandmother would be hurt and bewildered if you didn't wear the ring,' Gabriel said. 'Deep down, I do believe she thinks that it was always my intention to give my dearly beloved fiancée the ring that belonged to my mother. Indeed, she refused to accompany me down. Didn't want to spoil the special moment when I placed it tenderly on your waiting finger.'

'You're so cynical, Gabriel.'

He shrugged, took the box from her and flipped open the lid, then he removed the ring and circled it thoughtfully between his fingers. 'I don't even remember my mother wearing this,' he mused.

'That's really sad.'

'Is it?'

'Yes. It is.' She took the box from him and slipped the ring on her finger. 'This feels…weird.'

'Well, I don't suppose either of us ever imagined that we'd end up engaged.'

'Very funny.'

'It might be a charade but I don't want my grand-mother suspecting anything. Above all else, we have to be convincing.'

'That's going to take some effort,' Abby murmured lightly, but her heart did a little flip as she held out her hand, twirling it around and admiring the charming old-fashioned setting in which was nestled one perfect diamond surrounded by a circle of tinier ones. The ring she had returned to Jason had been a stark, modern piece. She had thought she liked it but, compared to this, it was forgettable.

'Why?'

'You? Me? We're a good team when I'm working for you…'

'And this is no different,' Gabriel said, shifting so that he was looking at her profile. And a remarkably delicate profile it was as well.

She was hot, tired and quite probably dazed, yet he would never have guessed as she stared serenely out to the darkened landscape.

Feeling his eyes on her, Abby remained quite still, but she had to make an effort to breathe normally.

'We get to my proposition.' Gabriel broke the silence, although he kept his eyes on her averted face, mesmerised by the smoothness of her cheeks and the silkiness of her hair which had unravelled during their journey so that, normally sleek and tidy, there were strands blowing across her cheeks in the lazy, nighttime breeze.

He resisted an insane urge to brush them off her face.

Abby turned slowly to look at him, thankful that the relative darkness hid her expression because she had no idea what to expect.

'Like I said to you, I am deeply grateful for your agreement in helping me, Abby. Trust me, I know it's beyond your remit. But I think it's important that we keep this on a business footing, and here's what I propose. You've told me about your parents and about your father cashing in all his bonds so that he can take your mother on a recuperative cruise. I'm guessing that that must leave him in a somewhat vulnerable state, financially.'

'It's nothing he can't handle.' Or so he'd assured her worriedly six months ago, when he had told her what he planned to do.

'Being financially stretched when you're a certain age is always something a guy finds tough to handle,' Gabriel said with assertion. 'So here's what I propose. I give you the equivalent of what he has had to invest in this trip. In other words, I restore his finances to rude health. Let's be honest here, Abby, if your father's pension is exhausted, he's going to be left in a very precarious state, and that kind of stress is the worst sort.'

'Yes, it is,' Abby said calmly. Part of her wanted to turn his offer down flat because it went against every grain of pride inside her, but why should she?

He was right. What he'd asked her to do was way beyond her remit and why should she be the eternally well-behaved secretary, willing to go the distance when it came to sacrifice?

Looking back, she realised that she'd done a lot over the past two years that was beyond her remit, even though she was paid handsomely.

Everyone in the company was paid handsomely but she was one of the few who worked long into the night because Gabriel was a tough taskmaster with almost no comprehension when it came to putting private life ahead of work.

Without complaint, she'd arranged his love life, booking venues, buying trinkets and sorting out flowers when relationship after relationship had crashed and burned. In other words, doing stuff she fundamentally disagreed with. And she'd done it all without complaint because she'd been vulnerable and still hurting when she'd come to London and she'd embraced the wonderful job she'd landed with the enthusiasm of someone embracing a miracle cure.

And, of course, the pay had been enough to keep her there, working like a bee without digging her heels in.

But now...

'I accept,' she said simply, linking her fingers on her stomach and maintaining eye contact, enough to see a flicker of surprise cross his lean features. 'You expected me to argue, didn't you?'

'It crossed my mind.'

'Would we get this all legally documented?'

'Since when have I ever been known to go back on my word?' Gabriel was outraged that she could suspect any such thing. She might be a romantic at heart but, when it came to him, she was all business, wasn't she?

'I suppose the fewer people who know the better,' Abby voiced aloud. 'I don't have all the details of my father's finances...'

'Spare me the boring details,' Gabriel drawled with a sweep of his hand. 'A general overview will do just fine. I'll take it and double whatever it is. In exchange, you become the perfect fiancée, convincing enough to persuade my grandmother that her grandson has found himself the ideal woman.'

'That's a very generous offer,' Abby told him politely. 'And, now that that's sorted, I'd like to lay down a few ground rules in connection with this...er...situation.'

Gabriel raised his eyebrows and she looked at him steadily, trying hard not to focus on the way the over-

head veranda light—an ornamental hanging lantern that
shed precious little light and made the sitting area feel
ridiculously romantic—emphasised the strong, perfect
lines of his face.

'I'm all ears,' he said wryly. She had to be the first
woman not to go quietly with the flow. It seemed that
he had misjudged the stubborn strength of her personality simply because she'd been the perfect PA, never
questioning his orders but just getting on with it. Or
maybe, he mused, he'd sensed that quiet strength all
along but was only now seeing it first-hand because of
the situation in which they found themselves.

He liked it. He was accustomed to women who
tripped over him and were always eager to please. He
wondered, not for the first time, he realised, what the
guy-she-wouldn't-talk-about had been like and suddenly, out of the blue, it struck him that he might rather
like this fake engagement. He was curious about her and
he was even more curious now that he had glimpsed
previously unseen depths to her. It always paid to know
your employees, he reasoned. In this situation, thrown
together and pretending to an intimacy they didn't actually share, he might get to explore those tantalising
hidden depths: as a newly engaged couple, they could
hardly politely talk about the weather and the state of
the economy when they were with his grandmother.
She would expect familiarity and, bearing that in mind,
who knew what gems might be revealed about his perfectly behaved PA?

'We're going to have to get back to normal life in a
week, and I'd like there to be no awkwardness between
us. I mean…' She hesitated. 'Things changed a bit with

all that Lucy business. I never meant to get involved in your private life but I found myself in it.'

'You're making a big deal of it. No need.'

'There's every need!' Abby told him fiercely. 'One minute everything is fine between us...'

'Who says things aren't fine now? Because I know a bit more about you, apart from the fact that your favourite colour appears to be grey?'

Abby reddened but stood her ground. 'Whatever pretending we do is just for your grandmother's sake. I mean, I'm not going to play at being girlish or giggly, and I won't be staring up at you with eyes like saucers, hanging onto your every word.'

'I'm disappointed. How did you know that that's exactly what I look for in the women I date?'

'You may not look for it, Gabriel, but I've seen enough of those women to know that it's how they treat you. As though you're the next best thing to sliced bread.'

Gabriel had to concede that she had a point. 'So, no saucer eyes. On the other hand, like I said, we're going to have to put on a convincing show, so positioning yourself as far away from me as possible and looking as though you're only there under sufferance isn't going to do. Let's not forget that we have an arrangement—one that will benefit your family considerably.'

Abby nodded jerkily. 'I'm aware of that. Of course I'm not going to spend my time scowling and making snide comments. There's one more thing—I'm not going to be sharing a room with you.'

Gabriel burst out laughing and looked at her with open amusement. 'What do you think we might get up to when the lights go down?' The casualness of his voice was belied by a tightening in his groin, the same shocking surge of his libido that had afflicted him when he had imagined her sprawled naked across his bed.

Abby tilted her chin defiantly.

'I don't think there's any danger of that happening, Abby,' he said.

'No, of course not! I didn't say that there would be. I'm your PA, and I suspect we both know very well that we could share the same bed and nothing would happen! It would be ludicrous to think otherwise! But I wouldn't feel comfortable with that sort of situation, even though—and I can't stress this *enough*—nothing would happen in a month of Sundays!'

Her skin burned and she was tingling all over. The silence that greeted this fiery outburst built and built until it was a solid, throbbing weight between them.

She'd seen this ploy a thousand times, the silence that stretched like a piece of elastic pulled to breaking point until whoever was with Gabriel was prompted into saying stuff he or she might not have planned to say.

Now, as the silence grew, she found herself doing the very same thing, and she could have kicked herself when she heard herself telling him that he wasn't her type, but that that was hardly the point.

'I think you know where I'm going with this…' She came to a stumbling halt.

'Oh, completely.' Gabriel waved one hand. 'Actually, what I meant was that my grandmother would no more think of throwing us into the same room than she would think of hot-air ballooning over the Ivory Coast. Don't forget that she's in her early eighties. She harks back to an era when men courted young ladies and the most outrageous thing a courting couple could do would be to hold hands.'

'Surely she must know that those women you date are slightly more adventurous, maybe looking for a little more than holding hands?' Abby said snidely and Gabriel's eyebrows shot up.

'"Those women"?'

Abby caught herself and remembered just who he was. She didn't think she'd ever passed judgement on any of the women who had entered and left his life with precious little breathing space between them.

'You mentioned that she had met a couple of them...'
'Those women?'

'Okay.' She shrugged and slanted a sideways glance at him, which was a mistake, because he was looking directly at her and, once their eyes met, she found she couldn't unglue hers from his face. 'Maybe I've put them into a box but everyone has opinions. I'm no different.'

'I would never have guessed that you had opinions about anything, aside from what might be happening on the work front.'

'That's insulting,' Abby said coldly, stung because in that throwaway remark he had somehow made her seem dull and uninteresting.

'No, it's not. It's the persona you've spent two years being at pains to cultivate,' Gabriel told her with equal cool.

'I didn't think I was employed to shoot my mouth off about everything under the sun.'

'Nor were you employed to be a saint.'

'Would you have appreciated it if I'd told you what I thought of some of those women?'

'Quite possibly not,' Gabriel murmured softly. 'But,

now we've strayed onto the subject, why don't you get it off your chest?'

Abby bit down what she wanted to say. He was being provocative. He did that extremely well and she wasn't going to take the bait. She wasn't going to let the sultry warmth over here, the fact that she was no longer in her comfort zone, go to her head.

'Perhaps we should head inside,' she said primly and Gabriel laughed softly.

'Running scared?'

'Scared of what, Gabriel?' Her heart was thumping inside her and the palms of her hands were sweaty. If it wasn't so shadowy, she knew he would be able to see just how much he was getting to her.

'Speaking your mind.'

'Not at all. I just think your grandmother might be waiting for us.'

'With simmering excitement... Naturally she won't be expecting us to rush inside after I've put the ring on your finger, but far be it from me to keep you out here against your will.' He vaulted upright and then held out his hand to help her to her feet. It was a perfectly normal gesture which Abby pretended not to notice.

Walking ahead of him, she had the advantage of being able to create some distance between them, but that was instantly wiped out by the fact that she was very conscious of him watching her from behind. She'd no curves. Not like the women he dated. Would he be making comparisons?

That thought had never crossed her mind but crossed it now, and she was burning all over when she pushed open the kitchen door to find Ava sitting at the kitchen table. Simmering excitement sprang to mind.

'I thought of coming outside but I didn't want to disturb you love birds...'

Abby grimaced and then, shocking her to the core, she felt the weight of Gabriel's hand slide under her hair to cup the nape of her neck. He stepped towards her and dropped a kiss on the side of her neck.

In a whoosh, the breath left her body and her legs turned to jelly.

'I'm too old to be a love bird,' Gabriel said wryly, absently trailing a finger along Abby's collarbone. Her hair was as soft as silk as it brushed against his knuckles and her skin was just as soft. 'That's for teenagers.'

'Love keeps you young at heart,' Ava responded, positively glowing with satisfaction. 'Wouldn't you agree, Abby? Men can be so practical, especially that grandson of mine! Women love to be romanced. Maybe,' she chided, 'That's why you've taken so long to settle down! Now, let me see that ring on your finger. You have no idea how happy it makes me knowing that I won't be going to my grave thinking that Gabriel hasn't settled down.'

Abby quailed and then clasped her hands together. 'It *has* taken a while,' she murmured snidely. 'Probably because he *does* lack a romantic soul. In fact, I would say that he's just the sort who would let his long-suffering PA arrange his love life for him because he can't be bothered to make an effort. If *that* isn't lacking in romance, then I don't know *what* is.'

Subtly she moved away from that disturbing hand on her neck and went to sit next to Ava on the sofa. Unless Gabriel decided to sit on her lap, at least she would be free from any further suffocating expressions of phoney tenderness. She added with saccharin sweetness, payback for being plunged into unknown territory by her charismatic, unpredictable and altogether way too charming boss, 'Some might even say that he can be a bit of a bore with his emphasis on work, work, work...'

She couldn't resist a sidelong glance at Gabriel who raised his eyebrows and grinned.

'Which is why,' he purred, 'I'm a lucky man to have found just the right woman to take me away from all that.' Instead of doing what he should have done, which was to sit on the single chair on the opposite side of the coffee table, he strolled towards the back of the sofa so that he was standing directly behind Abby.

Still smiling at Ava, she stiffened and was hardly surprised when he rested both hands on her shoulders and kneaded her tender skin. Held captive with nowhere to go but to remain seated and endure the pressure of his fingers, Abby zoned out as Ava chatted about Gabriel, about how pleased his parents would have been, that they were looking down now and would be thrilled, and about wedding ideas.

Her entire brain, her entire *being*, was focused on what those long, clever, bronzed fingers were doing to her.

Electrical currents she hadn't known existed were zinging responses through her body. She was burning up and between her legs a treacherous pool of liquid heat was forcefully reminding her that she was a woman.

She knew that she croaked something when the conversation turned to wedding dresses but too much of her energy was being spent warding off her body's response to Gabriel's uninvited attentions.

Her breasts felt heavy. She was appalled to think that

what she really wanted to do was relax into Gabriel's devastating touch. Thank goodness the man couldn't get into her head and read her thoughts.

Her head was spinning but it cleared with surprising speed when she heard Ava say brightly, reaching out to place a small, warm hand on her arm, 'I've got my girl to get the room ready for you. It's the blue room, Gabriel. I'll walk up with you both.'

CHAPTER FIVE

GIRL? *WHAT* GIRL?

Alvira, apparently, the daily help who appeared to be as efficient as she was inconspicuous and who had been hard at it getting their room ready.

For a few seconds after Ava's announcement, Abby had somehow misunderstood what had been said. Or maybe she'd siphoned off chunks of the conversation because her nerves were all over the place.

Ava was an elderly woman with old-fashioned values and, as Gabriel had confidently pointed out, would be horrified at having her grandson share a bedroom with a woman under her roof.

That misconception skidded to an abrupt stop the minute the bedroom door was pushed open and Abby's eyes were inexorably drawn to two cases on the king-sized four-poster bed.

Gabriel's was just the right shade of battered tan to indicate a super-wealthy guy who didn't care how much of a beating his expensive leather holdall took.

And hers, functional, lightweight and easily identifiable because of the orange strap she had tied around it. Although anyone who mistakenly might have carried it away with them would have returned it fast enough once opened because all she had packed was an assortment of sober work clothes, with two tops that could elevate the black skirts for evening wear, and two pairs of jeans just in case she managed to get some time off from their busy schedule.

Her mouth fell open.

She tried to catch Gabriel's eye but he had inconveniently positioned himself by the huge window and was staring out with his back to her, so Abby turned to Ava, who winked at her.

'I may be old,' she whispered, in a voice that easily carried to Gabriel—who still didn't turn around, Abby was infuriated to note, , 'But I'm not so ancient that I don't understand the ways of the world.'

'Ways of the world?' Abby parroted faintly.

'You young people naturally want to share a room and I'm perfectly happy with that. You're going to be Gabriel's wife. That's enough for me.'

Excruciating guilt swamped Abby. 'Really, Ava, I have the utmost respect for you and I wouldn't dream of…of sharing a room with…er…your grandson.' Just saying those words felt surreal and made her want to pass out. 'And I'm sure Gabriel would agree with me.' She edged towards her suitcase, preparatory to grabbing it and running for any other room that happened to have a bed in it. The house was enormous. There would be no shortage of spare bedrooms.

Eventually, Gabriel turned round and strolled towards Abby, proceeding to put his arm round her shoulders. 'Abby's right,' he said gravely. 'We are more than happy to sleep in separate bedrooms but of course, if you've gone to the trouble of getting Alvira to prepare this one for us…'

'You would make an old lady very happy to use this room. You know it's always been reserved for you, Gabriel.' She pointed to two shelves by the door. 'And I've popped some framed pictures of you there because I thought the woman you were going to marry might want to see you as a young boy. He was just so beautiful, Abby.'

Her eyes glistened and another shard of guilt pierced through Abby, who smiled and looked obediently at an adolescent Gabriel looking moody and beautiful in various different settings. As a baby, he'd been beautiful, as a toddler he'd been beautiful and growing up he'd clearly just carried on being beautiful. Every photo she'd laid eyes on thus far was testament to someone ridiculously blessed in the looks department.

He would have been breaking hearts from the age of thirteen, she thought acidly, and he hadn't stopped since then.

'Lovely,' Abby said. 'Super.'

'Now, don't you two go rushing to get up early in the morning! I know Gabriel mentioned something about having to work. Didn't you, Gabriel?'

'A bit.' Gabriel bent to give his grandmother a peck on the cheek, towering over the diminutive Ava, yet as gentle as Abby had ever seen him. The look he gave Ava was so full of affection that a lump formed in Abby's throat and she recognised why he had been so desperate to persuade her into this charade.

Even bustling and clearly excited, there was a frailty about the elderly woman that made sense of the warnings Gabriel had had from her doctor.

'But not too much, I hope,' she chided, looking at him anxiously. 'You work too hard. It's bad for you.

I'm just glad you found yourself a good woman who's spirited enough to tell you what I've been telling you for years! My dear.' She turned to Abby. 'You're just right for my grandson. I could tell that just as soon as I realised that you weren't going to lie down and pander to him. That lad sometimes has quite an ego.'

Gabriel burst out laughing and Abby said, sotto voce but still loud enough for them both to hear, 'Tell me about it.'

She smiled and escorted Ava to the door but the smile dropped from her face the second the door was shut.

'How *could* you?' Arms folded, Abby spun round to glare at Gabriel. 'How *could you* let this happen?'

'I had no idea my grandmother was that liberal-minded,' Gabriel mused without, Abby felt, the right amount of horror at the fact that they had been shoved into one bedroom, a situation she had no intention of enduring.

She watched as he strolled towards his suitcase and began extracting some clothes from it.

'What sort of answer is that?' Abby demanded.

'She's always had a lot to say on the subject of those *easy women* who seem happy to jump in and out of bed with me. The single one time I came here with... Wait... No, can't quite recall her name... Sexy thing—long curling dark hair, legs up to her armpits...'

'Gabriel!' Abby exploded with frustration and he raised both hands in mock surrender.

'I honestly didn't think that she would put us together, Abby.' He looked at her with lazy, brooding intensity, his long, lean body relaxed. If she was seething, then he appeared to be the epitome of calm. 'I could only go on past history, and four years ago she was

quite Victorian in her insistence that the woman I had
brought over was housed in the furthest bedroom from
my own. She likes you.'

'I have no idea how you've reached that conclusion
but I'm not sharing this bedroom with you.'

'Yes, Abby,' Gabriel said calmly. 'You are.'

Abby gaped, lost for words. All professional cool
had disappeared. She was frazzled, tired and so out of
her depth that she would have needed more than a life
belt to save her. And through all this Gabriel was as
cool as a cucumber, his dark eyes gazing at her with
utter cool.

'When I told you that we would have to be convincing, I meant it. My grandmother might be old but she's
not an idiot and you can see for yourself how much
she's clinging to this engagement. If she thinks that
it's been engineered for her benefit, she's going to be
a thousand times more upset than when she finds out
that we're no longer an item. So storming out of this
bedroom with your suitcase in your hand isn't going to
happen. Simple as that.'

'I'm afraid you can't tell me what to do.' But she
heard the thread of desperation in her voice.

'And I very much hate to disappoint you, but I can.
We have a deal, don't forget. You will receive a substantial amount of money for what you've agreed to do.' He
raked his fingers through his hair. 'It's a big bedroom,'
he pointed out.

'It's a big bedroom with just the one bed,' Abby
blurted, and he shot her a slow, curling smile that made
the blood rush to her hairline.

'And?'

'What do you mean *and*?'

'Do you think that we are incapable of sharing a bed without sex occurring?'

'There's no need to be coarse!' Abby all but wailed.

'I understand that you're out of your depth and floundering…'

Abby looked away, because she couldn't deny it. Her heart was beating like a sledgehammer and the palms of her hands were sweaty. All she could see was the threatening contours of the four-poster bed, the puffy pillows, the silk throw. It was a vision of intimacy that filled her with terror.

Out of her depth? That had to be the understatement of the century.

'I'm more than happy to take the floor, if you would feel safer.'

Abby cringed. 'It's not that I wouldn't feel safe.'

'No,' Gabriel said thoughtfully. 'We've already had the long discussion about the fact that you could share a bed with me naked and you wouldn't be aroused in any way shape or form.'

'I never said that!'

'Are you telling me that you *would* be aroused?'

'Stop playing games with me, Gabriel!' she cried, and he immediately looked contrite.

'We could keep going over this until we bored each other into deep REM, but I've no idea what the point of that would be, so I'm going to have a shower. I'm hot and tired, as you no doubt are as well.' He began unbuttoning his shirt and she looked away, horrified that her well-ordered, predictable working relationship with her boss had come to this.

'Would you like to have the bathroom first?' he asked, mid-unbuttoning.

Polite, she thought a little wildly. He was being perfectly polite. They had somehow ended up in an unforeseen situation and he was keeping his calm and acting like an adult while she was going into meltdown.

He was right: they were here and she couldn't storm off with her suitcase to find herself one of those guest rooms, of which there were plenty. She wasn't just doing this out of the goodness of her heart, which would at least have given her the right to call the whole thing off, even though she knew deep down, having met his grandmother, that she wouldn't have.

She had signed up to a deal that would help her father. He would surely be worried sick about money as he and her mother cruised their way round the world on a trip that would gradually eat up all his savings and leave them on a much reduced pension. He was doing it for her mother, but if Abby could help her father then she would do so in a heartbeat.

So her rights when it came to calling the whole thing off were non-existent.

She would just have to salvage some of her composure and not go to pieces. She took a few deep breaths, and when she told him that he could go ahead her voice was as normal as his had been.

'And I apologise,' she said, 'if I overreacted. This is a very strange situation for me, and naturally I'm not one hundred percent comfortable with it.'

Gabriel thought that she looked like a woman on the verge of a nervous breakdown. Shorn of every scrap of her PA's façade, she was human all the way through, and he couldn't deny that he was enjoying this side of her, the ultra-feminine side that she had been at pains to conceal.

'Understood.' He turned away, but in his mind's eye he retained the image of her pink-cheeked, calm, grey eyes stormy and glittering, prissy clothes slightly askew and hair desperate to break free of its restraints.

Feminine. It was a word he had never associated with her but it best described her now. She was utterly and defiantly feminine.

Abby watched until the bathroom door was safely shut behind him and she could hear the running of the shower, then she moved at speed.

She didn't take time out to appreciate the cool beauty of the bedroom, which really was enormous, including as it did a seating area with two deep chairs and a little table on which a few magazines had been placed. The colours were neutral and calming, and the voile at the windows gave it a tropical feel, but all of those details were lost on her as she hastily began stripping the bed, removing two of the pillows and getting rid of the top flat sheet so that she could hobble together a sleeping arrangement for Gabriel on the floor.

She was sitting on one of the deep chairs when he eventually emerged from the shower. She couldn't have been more relieved that she had done what she had because he emerged with just some loose tracksuit bottoms on. No top. No comfy bedroom slippers.

Abby's mouth went dry. She stared, looked away, stared again and then spread her arms wide as he took in his new sleeping arrangement.

'You've been busy, I see,' he drawled, opening one of the drawers and extracting a tee shirt. He kept a stash of clothes in the room permanently and he slipped it on now as he cast a jaundiced eye at what had to be the most unappetising makeshift bed he had ever seen.

She could kid herself that he was going to sleep there, but she was wrong. His offer to take the floor had been polite at best. She had been on the point of exploding with nerves and it had been the only thing on the table to ease her mind. However, she would just have to appreciate that the floor was not conveniently carpeted, not that that would have made a whole lot of difference. It was cool marble, very pretty to look at but hardly good bedding fodder. The huge silk rug did nothing to help matters.

'You did offer...'

Gabriel grunted and pulled out his laptop, which gave Abby some measure of hope that he was going to do the decent thing and vacate the bedroom so that he could go and work somewhere else in the house.

With a little start, she realised that it was only the sight of the laptop that had brought her back down to earth with a bump.

He was her *boss*! So far had she gone since they'd arrived in Seville, she'd almost forgotten!

They hadn't discussed work once, not that there had been a lot of time, but still...

It was why she had come on this trip in the first place! Instead, here she was. Guilty grey eyes skittered away from the tantalising sight of her powerfully built boss clad in nothing but tracksuit bottoms and an old, soft tee shirt. The same guilty grey eyes travelled down to his feet and then back up, only to race past the telltale bulge in the bottoms that seemed to advertise that he was as well built there as he was everywhere else.

'I'll use the bathroom now, if you don't mind.' She leapt to her feet, practically falling in her haste to get out of the bedroom.

'Why would I mind?'

'Good idea to do some work now,' Abby gabbled as she opened her suitcase and pointedly turned away from him to search out the stupidly sexy lingerie she had brought.

Sexy lingerie and sexy underwear were her little secret pleasures. On the outside, she was perfectly happy with jeans and jumpers, and grey, black and navy-blue for work, but ever since her break-up with Jason she had quietly rebelled against the good-girl image he had had of her.

'You're a lovely girl,' he had said in just the sort of patronising voice that made her blood boil. 'And you'll make some lucky man a great wife, but I think I need someone a little more adventurous…'

He had found that adventurous lady fast enough. Indeed, rumour had it that he had encountered quite a few of those.

But, in the wake of Jason's backhanded compliment, Abby had quietly rebelled through her choice of underwear. She'd ditched sensible, 'good girl, you'll make some lucky guy a great wife' underwear and cotton nighties and gone wicked.

Never had she regretted that impulse until now as she clutched the silky burgundy piece of nothing she had brought to sleep in, and the thong.

Gabriel wasn't even looking in her direction. 'You have a point,' he said absently, scrolling down whatever he was reading. 'I think I'm going to have to do some work, because from the sounds of it my dear Grandmama has chosen to reinterpret what I told her about having to deal with a couple of clients while I was over here.'

Abby had been creeping stealthily towards the bathroom and now, as she slipped through the door, she said with airy insouciance, 'Brilliant idea.' And just in case he was in any danger of forgetting the balance of their relationship under the weight of unforeseen circumstance, 'And you can email anything you'd like me to do.'

'Why would I do that?' He glanced at her to see that she was peering round the door at him, modesty personified. Did it ever occur to her that all that modesty could be as much of a turn-on as if she'd decided to shed her clothes and perform a pole dance?

'What do you mean?'

'Why would I email you when we're sharing the same space and I can just sit and tell you face to face?'

'Because,' Abby said a little desperately, 'Your grandmother is going to think it odd if we're supposed to be an item and yet we're going through reports and getting up to date on a client list.'

Gabriel stood up and tucked his laptop neatly under his arm. Abby breathed a sigh of profound relief as she shut the bathroom door and began running a bath.

She could afford to relax. If there was one thing she knew about Gabriel, it was this—when he began focusing on work, he could be involved for hours. He never did anything in half-measures, especially when it came to work. That laptop under his arm was indication enough that she could have a relaxed bath and be safely tucked up before he returned to the bedroom.

In the morning, she would make sure she went into Seville and bought some sensible sleeping stuff, more for her own peace of mind than anything else.

For the first time since she'd arrived at the villa,

Abby took time out as she lay in the bubbly bath really to observe her surroundings.

The bathroom was huge and very modern. The shower was a walk-in, big enough to fit several people, and the bath tub was likewise oversized. Cool white complemented azure touches here and there. The towels on the heated towel rail were big, fluffy and snow-white. She could have been in a five-star hotel, which made sense, considering the villa was not used very often by anyone bar Ava.

Abby's mind drifted this way and that. Whenever it touched on the four-poster bed awaiting her, it reared up like a frightened horse facing an obstacle it couldn't surmount.

It was as silent as the grave as she finally drained the tub and then cleared the condensation from the bathroom mirror to stare at her reflection: bright eyed, skin pink and dewy, hair damp because, try as she had, she had not been able to keep it completely dry.

She looked down at the sexy short nightie that barely skirted her thighs and quickly slipped on the bathrobe provided on the back of the door.

Fingers riffling her hair, she pushed open the bathroom door and stopped short.

'You're out,' Gabriel drawled from where he was sprawled on the bed. 'I was about to send in the armed forces to make sure you hadn't come to any harm.'

'What are you doing here?'

'Working.' He held up the laptop and waved it.

'This is no place to work!' Suddenly remembering what she was wearing, and weak at the knees with relief that she hadn't made the mistake of prancing out in her next-to-nothing nightie, Abby yanked the belt of the bathrobe tightly around her. 'And why are you on that bed?'

Gabriel sat up and linked his fingers on his stomach. She'd pulled that belt so tightly around her that he was surprised she could carry on breathing but she hadn't got there fast enough. He'd seen something he would never have imagined possible in a million years. His PA, his *perfect* PA, who did her utmost to make sure every strand of hair was in place, had a liking for sexy underwear!

That glimpse...it had fired him up like a jolt of pure adrenaline.

A short, silky little number in a hot red colour, and slender legs that would make the pulse of any red-blooded male go into instant overdrive.

It was almost a punishable crime that she had spent the past two years concealing those from sight!

Gabriel had always had a hard and fast rule never to mix business with pleasure, but right now that rule was in serious danger of going out the window.

'Which question would you like me to answer first?'

'Don't be funny, Gabriel!'

'I can't help it when you're standing there with steam pouring out of your ears.'

'You said you'd be downstairs working!'

'I never said any such thing. That must have been the result of your fertile imagination. This is as good a place to work as any, and I'm in this bed because there's no way I'm sleeping on the floor.'

'But you promised!' Riven with uncertainty, Abby remained where she was, hovering by the bathroom door. She couldn't look at him, yet she couldn't resist. He was so superbly, aggressively *masculine*, sprawled on that bed with his legs crossed, half-propped up with the pillows squashed behind him, his fabulous dark eyes boring holes into her and turning her brain to mush.

'I suggested that it might be an option,' Gabriel corrected. 'That was before I worked out just how uncomfortable the ice-cold marble ground was going to be.'

Abby automatically followed his gaze to the make-shift bed she had erected, which was still in place, untouched. How had things spiralled so completely out of control? She'd worked so hard at putting together a shield that was strong enough to weather anything thrown at it, any Jason who might bounce along and try to wreck her life again, and she positively *hated* Gabriel right now for dismantling it in the space of a few fraught hours.

'Fine,' she said tautly. 'I'll take the floor. This isn't my house and I should have known better than to have asked you to do the honours.'

She gingerly tiptoed across the floor, which suddenly seemed as broad and as limitless as the Norfolk broads, then angled herself under the sheet, trying hard not to grimace at the unspeakable discomfort.

She wanted to burst into tears. Instead, she squeezed her eyes shut tightly, and was so absorbed in trying not to move, even though her body was already beginning to ache, that she didn't sense Gabriel's approach until she was being lifted into the air and heaved over his shoulder as he walked back to the bed with her, dropping her on the mattress and then towering at the side of the bed with his arms folded.

'This is ludicrous,' he growled, while Abby frantically tried to shuffle into a sitting position whilst keeping the bathrobe in place. Appalled, she eyed her naked thighs, and with a yelp of horror she dove under the duvet and then proceeded to glare at him with all the ferocity at her command.

Never had she felt so mortified. Never had she wanted the ground to open, swallow her up and disgorge her somewhere very, very far away.

'Neither of us is going to sleep on the floor,' Gabriel said in a voice that brooked no debate, never mind argument. 'It would be a recipe for a visit to the local hospital. It's physically impossible to sleep on this floor, and not only am I *not* going to jeopardise my health but I have a duty of care to you as my employee and I will simply not allow it, Abby.'

He strode towards the linen on the ground, swept the lot up and dumped it all on the bed. Then he proceeded to lie down and grope for the discarded laptop so that he could carry on where he had left off.

While Abby fumed and seethed, hunched on her side and staring at the wall, she tried to block him out of her mind completely.

Abby had no idea when or even how she managed to fall asleep but she did.

Next to her, Gabriel had managed to sit in front of his computer for over an hour and a half without seeing anything at all. He was so acutely aware of the body next to him on the bed that it took almost superhuman effort not to turn and look.

That nightgown.

Who'd have thought?

When at last he quietly switched off his laptop and turned, it was to see that she had shifted in her sleep. She'd kicked off most of the duvet so that her slender leg rested on top. The bathrobe had likewise dislodged.

Of course, it would be ridiculously hot sleeping with it on, and without waking she had tried to wriggle out of it so that it was half-on, half-off, just enough off to reveal the dip of her cleavage and the peep of her nipple. Moonlight pouring through the window emphasised the pale softness of her skin.

Gabriel knew he should look away. He couldn't. Not yet. He was riveted by the sight of her and by that pink nipple. He closed his eyes and shuddered. Stifling a groan of frustration, he slipped out of the bed and headed straight to the shower.

This time it was going to have to be a cold one.

When Abby woke the following morning, the room was quiet and there was a space beside her where Gabriel had been. She could still see the indentation left by his body.

A glance at her mobile told her that it was already after nine, way later than she was accustomed to waking, which was good, because it left her no time to think about events that had happened the day before or to ruminate on the night she had spent in bed with her boss.

If this was going to be the pattern set, then she could live with it. It wasn't going to be great but it was obvious that he was sticking to his usual routine of working from very early in the morning. He'd once told her, in passing, that sleep was a waste of perfectly good working time. He'd been joking, but only half-joking, and now she hoped that he hadn't been joking at all, in which case she could look forward to seeing precious little of him in the bedroom.

Buoyed by that, Abby was less stressed as the day

progressed. Gabriel excused himself for a call which, he explained to his grandmother, was unavoidable.

'It's either that or I try and set up a series of meetings in Seville,' he said.

If he'd expected opposition, then he was mistaken, for Ava was only too happy to have Abby to herself.

'What if your grandmother starts asking me about wedding plans?' Abby hissed to him as she followed him out to the perfectly good office which he had shunned the night before, preferring instead to wreck her sleep by working in bed next to her.

'Use your imagination.' Gabriel looked down at her and lounged against the wall. 'You seem to have an excellent one when it comes to all sorts of scenarios.' Behind her, on the way to the kitchen, he spotted his grandmother who had paused to look at them fondly, clearly interpreting their body language as that of adoring lovers. They were certainly standing close to one another, Gabriel thought, but if only she could see the mutinous scowl on his beloved's face.

He grinned. 'I thought women enjoyed discussing wedding plans—the flowers…the dress…the extensive guest list of relatives who largely hate one another…'

'Very funny.' But she wanted to grin because of his dry tone of voice. 'That's incredibly sexist.'

'Please accept my apologies.' Gabriel was, unrepentant. 'If it's any consolation, there's nothing I would enjoy more than chatting to my grandmother about wedding plans.'

Abby's lips twitched and she tried and failed to stifle a giggle at the incongruous image of her over-the-top alpha male boss talking wedding plans with anyone.

'Don't look now,' he murmured, bending so that his

posture was now even more intimate, 'But we have an audience, and as you've been so good today so far, smiling, laughing, pretending to enjoy riveting anecdotes about my academic achievements…'

Staring up at him, Abby could scarcely breathe. The lazy charm in his voice, the teasing glitter in his eyes, that amused, crooked smile, all took her breath away. Never had she been so up close and personal with him before, not like this, and she was responding with every pore and fibre of her being.

'It would almost be a shame not to give my darling grandma something to really smile about, wouldn't it?'

He could breathe her in and the smell of her was filling his head: sweet, clean and strangely *innocent*. Hell, he'd never found it so damned difficult to think about work. The morning had been an exercise in low-level frustration and how to control it.

And now…

Gabriel didn't give her time to protest. He tipped her chin just as he lowered his head and he kissed her.

CHAPTER SIX

ABBY GASPED AGAINST his mouth, then her eyes were closing and her mouth opening up to the heady pleasure of his exploring tongue.

It was a long, lingering, sweetly seductive kiss. No rush, no hurry, but a kiss that took its time. She raised her hands, pressing them flat against his chest. She wanted to do so much more than that, though. She wanted to push them under his shirt, run them over every inch of his broad, hard chest. She wanted to go further, to dip her fingers beneath the waistband of his jeans, unzip them and find the erotic bulge of his manhood.

With a yelp, she came to her senses and gave him a determined shove.

She turned around and tried to look as casual as she could when her body was on the point of exploding. Ava was smiling with satisfaction.

'I was just on my way out into the garden,' she said. 'Why don't you come and join me, my dear, if that grandson of mine insists on working? You could have a swim in the pool. It's a wonderful day.'

'No swimsuit.' Abby shook her head ruefully because splashing around in the pool was relatively low on her agenda. It smacked of being on holiday and, whilst she wasn't exactly doing the kind of work she had come out to do, relaxing to that extent felt wrong.

'Gabriel,' Ava chided. 'Why didn't you tell Abby that there was a pool here? He made sure there was a pool here,' she confided, 'Because he was insistent that I get some daily exercise, but swimming's far too energetic for an old woman like me so it's just sitting there, unused, except when friends visit and bring their grandchildren with them.' She looked at Gabriel meaningfully. 'Some ladies are lucky enough to have grandchildren *and* great-grandchildren as well.'

'Let's not run before we can walk,' Gabriel commented wryly. 'No swimsuit...' He looked at Abby, head tilted to one side. 'Pity. My grandmother's right, it's a shame not to use the pool while we're here, and I would certainly feel far better if I knew you were having fun outside while I worked.'

'I'm happy to help with your work.' Abby turned to Ava. 'We've found that, incredibly, we work really well together! I'm a PA by profession, so I can get the hang of things fairly quickly, and when Gabriel's discussed work I've found that I just seem to catch on to what he's saying.'

'But you're not going to work while you're here,' Ava said firmly, and Gabriel strolled towards Abby, his eyes never leaving her face until she was remembering that brief kiss and burning up all over again.

'You're right, Grandmama.' He slung his arm around Abby's shoulders and pulled her close against him, then he dipped to kiss the top of her head, and for a few seconds breathed in that strangely seductive scent of hers, which had nothing to do with perfume but was the completely natural scent of soap and shampoo.

She was much slighter than any of the women he had ever dated, including Lucy, who was very tall and very rangy, and whilst he'd always assumed his type to be full-figured and tall he liked her smallness, liked the way it made him feel—as though she needed protecting.

Hilarious, considering she was as sharp as a tack.

Yet vulnerable.

That thought came from nowhere and lodged in his head, forcing him to analyse it. She was romantic, she was vulnerable and she'd had a terrible relationship with a guy who'd obviously dumped her, having built her expectations up towards a wedding with all the frills and lace that went with it.

Abby was still grinning but her jaw was beginning to ache from the effort.

'I don't think it's fair of me to abandon my fiancée because I need to close a multi-million-pound deal.'

'Oh, you won't be *abandoning* me, *darling*. I *quite* understand! Don't forget I'm a PA, as you know, and I've seen first-hand how *driven* some men can be when it comes to work! I've become quite accustomed to my boss forgetting everything when he's in the middle of a big deal!'

She edged away from Gabriel's embrace, but not far, because he settled his grip ever firmer, anchoring her next to him. 'Between you and me,' she said to Ava in a woman-to-woman, confiding tone, 'My boss can be a huge bore when it comes to work…'

'Tut, tut, I don't believe that for a second! Now, enough of this. You don't have a swimsuit, so I'm going to take you shopping. Show you the delights of Seville.'

He broke apart and held her at arm's length so that he could inspect her in such a leisurely fashion that Abby had to grit her teeth not to say something snappy to him. 'New wardrobe,' he said briskly.

'Gabriel, darling,' his grandmother said. 'I never thought I'd ever hear you volunteer to go shopping. You've always told me that it's your least favourite pastime, but I expect going shopping with the woman you love turns it into a pleasure.'

'I don't need any clothes, Gabriel.'

'Shh...' Gabriel placed one long, brown finger over her lips and smiled. 'You're far too proud. Jeans are all well and good, but I shall be taking you both to a couple of excellent restaurants while we're here and I'll want to show you off.'

Trapped, Abby mentally said goodbye to the remainder of her day. In a fog, she heard him invite his grandmother out for the excursion, but before she could get her hopes up that Ava might accompany them she heard his grandmother make her excuses.

What was wrong with her jeans, the handful of skirts she had brought over? She'd thought she'd be in conference rooms in front of her tablet. Was it her fault that that plan had been turned on its head?

Abby might indulge a secret desire for naughty in her underwear and her sexy night gowns, but that was where it ended. She'd grown up in a tiny village, the only child of doting parents, and she'd never been one to wear daring outfits. Her very traditional background had trained her to dress in a certain kind of way and she felt safe with that.

Besides, she'd never felt that she had the sort of figure to pull off small, tight clothes anyway. She'd always left that to well-endowed friends who'd been keen to display their assets.

She'd thought that that was what Jason had loved about her, her lack of showiness. She'd been wrong. Another woman might have reacted by changing her look, but Abby had had the confidence knocked out of her, and she had been happy to become even more re-tiring in her dress than she had been before.

'This is stupid,' were her opening words just as soon as they were in the four-wheel drive Gabriel had had delivered to the house the day before.

It was a beautiful day, sunny with a clear blue sky, but Abby was too busy fuming to enjoy the loveliness around her as the car slowly eased away from the villa and out of the compound onto open road.

'Is there any point in time when you're not going to argue with me?'

Abby reddened. 'I just don't need any clothes, and I can't afford to buy a new wardrobe.'

'Whoever said anything about you paying for it? You're doing me a favour. I will be writing the cheque.'

'I'm not doing you a favour. This is a transaction. A business transaction.' Earlier—with some embarrass-ment, because accepting money from someone, how-ever justifiable it might be, stuck in her throat—she had written down what she surmised her father would have spent on the recuperative round-the-world cruise with her mother.

She'd known roughly because he had discussed it with her months ago, on the proviso she said nothing to her mother.

'She'd worry,' her father had confided. 'And you know that's the last thing she should be doing.'

Then he'd named the sum and the blood had drained from Abby's face.

Well, Gabriel naturally hadn't batted an eyelid at the figure, because to him it was loose change. He had promptly doubled the figure she had given him and she knew that the online transfer of funds to her bank account had already been done.

So the business transaction was complete.

But a brand-new wardrobe wasn't part of any business transaction.

'And quibbling about it is going to make my grandmother suspicious. Not only do most women enjoy having clothes lavished on them...'

'I don't.'

'But my grandmother knows that I am exceedingly generous when it comes to women. It would strike her as odd that you've come over here in clothes better suited to an office, and she would be appalled if you refused to accept my largesse.'

'I'll pay you back.'

Gabriel didn't say anything. His mouth tightened and he continued driving until they approached the busy outskirts of the city. He found parking with ease, killed the engine and then turned to her.

'You're not going to pay me back, Abby, and you're going to stop acting like a badly behaved child.'

'That's not fair!'

'This is all part and parcel of our little *transaction*, the object of which was to ensure that my grandmother was relieved of all the stress that has seen her possibly reach for too many tablets.' He paused, eyes narrowed. 'Is this how you were with your ex?'

Abby was so shocked by the directness of his question that she could only stare at him, open-mouthed.

'Did you knock him back whenever he tried to do something for you?' Gabriel knew that he was pushing it, but he couldn't deny that he'd been curious about her past, curious enough now to barge straight past all 'no entry' signs.

'How *dare* you?'

'How dare I what? Ask you a simple question about your past?'

'It's none of your business what happened between Jason and myself!'

'Did you love him?' Gabriel asked gently.

It was the tone of his voice that did it. He'd moved from cool to tender in a heartbeat and it caught her on the hop.

Abby hadn't spoken to anyone about the break-up. Not really. She had put a brave face on it, smiled and pulled through and everyone had marvelled that she'd got her act together so well. One less thing for her parents to worry about, she had reasoned. Besides, she had always been private by nature. It hadn't been difficult to bury the hurt under silence and a stiff upper lip.

'It was a long time ago,' she said tightly.

'Tell me what happened.'

Abby opened her mouth to tell him that, actually, it was none of his business, but instead she gave a strangled little sound and looked away, biting down on her lip to keep the tumult of her emotions under control.

Gabriel had little time for female histrionics and uncontrolled sobbing jags. They always left him feeling uncomfortable. He was strangely moved to see that she was trying hard *not* to cry.

Instead of swiftly closing off the conversation, he said, 'Things that happen long ago can still cast long shadows. What happened?'

'We were childhood sweethearts, you could say.' Abby took a deep breath, blinked back the onset of tears and felt a certain release at opening up about something that, yes, had cast something of a shadow whether she cared to admit that or not. 'We grew up in the same small village in Somerset, Jason and I...' She slid a sideways glance at the big, overwhelming man sitting next to her, his body angled so that he was facing her. 'I bet you don't even know where that is, Gabriel.' She smiled and he returned the smile with a crooked one of his own.

'It rings a bell.'

'Well,' she laughed, 'It would be your nightmare destination. Everyone knows everyone else. We went out, and got more serious when we were seventeen. It never occurred to either of us that university might test the relationship, and it didn't. I went to do my IT course close by, and Jason went to Exeter University, but really he was back often and things seemed closer than ever between us. He said he thought that the girls at university were immature. Am I boring you?'

'Do I look bored?'

'I don't know why I'm telling you this.' She sighed and leaned back, her eyes half-closed.

'Because I'm your fiancé,' he teased and she smiled but didn't look at him or open her eyes. 'Carry on.'

'We got engaged. Everyone was excited—parents, friends, cousins, great-aunts...over the moon.' She looked at the finger where once she'd worn another engagement ring. It felt like a century ago that her heart had been broken, which made her realise that she was over it and had been for a lot longer than she'd thought. This was what happened when you verbalised, she thought wryly.

'I'd already got a job in the village, but we were planning on moving to Exeter, or maybe Southampton. But then Jason got a job in London working for one of the investment banks and everything just went pear-shaped after that.'

'Investment banks can do that to a person.'

'To you?'

'I don't succumb to lack of self-control,' Gabriel told her with scorching honesty. 'When I get involved with someone, it's because I choose to, and not because my head's been somehow turned in the heat of the moment. Is that what happened?'

'He was suddenly in demand by lots of women, and they weren't the immature variety he'd met at university. Bit by bit our relationship was chipped away until there was nothing left of it. I barely saw him. When I did, he no longer had time for me. I'd become the old, comfortable shoe he was no longer interested in wearing.'

Self-pity swamped her and she didn't stop the tear from trickling down her cheek. When Gabriel pushed a handkerchief into her hand, she took it, still without looking at him, and dashed the stupid tear off her cheek.

'So that's my tale of woe.' She turned to look at him. God, he was beautiful. Especially now, when the harsh lines of his face were relaxed. Her grey eyes drifted to his sensual mouth and lingered.

Gabriel wondered whether she was aware of what she

was doing, of the directness of her gaze, of what she was capable of rousing in a guy with that look.

'Okay.' Abby roused herself from the trance-like torpor that had suddenly settled over her. 'I see your point about the wardrobe but I'm not going to be letting you buy me the sort of clothes the women you go out with wear.'

Gabriel grinned and pushed open his car door, then he stepped out into the balmy sunshine and circled to open the passenger door.

'You're the woman I plan on marrying,' he said in a low, husky voice. 'I wouldn't dream of allowing you out of the house in anything but modest dresses with high necks and low hems.'

You're the woman I plan on marrying...

For a few seconds, something swept through her, a tidal rush of colourful scenarios in which those words actually came from the heart, and she was appalled by the very fact that she'd given in to wild imaginings like that.

'Then isn't it brilliant that I'm not that girl?' she asked tartly. 'Because I may not be heading down the aisle with the micro-minis but I certainly won't be going for the granny look.'

She felt buoyant. Confession was obviously good for the soul, even if it was a confession delivered to the last person on earth she'd ever expected to deliver it to.

She relaxed, looked around her and let his words wash over her as he told her about the city, a potted history of the place.

The Moorish architecture was there in the graceful arches and the stucco he pointed out. Then came the churches and the palaces. They meandered, and she looked and listened. The city was charming, the sepia colours reminiscent of a bygone era. They wandered through an enchanting maze of streets that were cool and whitewashed, and by the time they hit the shopping area Abby was as relaxed as she never thought she would be, given the circumstances.

Housed in ornate old buildings, the selection of boutiques from the outside seemed to offer everything and a thrill of pure feminine pleasure rippled through her.

'I'm better off shopping on my own,' she said firmly. She had to remind herself that this was all make-believe. They weren't the happy loved-up couple doing everything together. 'If you point me in the right direction, I can meet you in, say, an hour, maybe a bit longer. And, now that your grandmother isn't here, we can maybe discuss work. I feel like I'm playing truant and I'm a little uncomfortable with that.'

'Well, we wouldn't want that, would we?' He gave her the name of a restaurant, pointed out where she should be walking, and told her that it was famous so, if she ended up lost, she would easily be directed to the right place.

He walked off and she felt...strangely bereft.

It was as though he had left a hole behind him and she had to shake her head to clear the silly feeling away.

He'd left her his credit card and she stared at it...then she gave in to purely girlish anticipation and pushed open the glass door to boutique number one.

Gabriel glanced at his watch. His grandmother's driver had ferried her to friends for the evening.

'You two love birds can enjoy yourselves without

having to entertain an old lady!' she had carolled as she'd been ushered into the back of the car.

On some fronts, this was cause for some unease to Gabriel. Yes, it was good that she was clearly in high spirits and whatever depression she had been suffering had been temporarily shelved. However, the gusto with which she had embraced the phoney engagement surpassed anything he had foreseen. Whilst previously the ends had soundly justified the means, he was now beginning to see the difficulties that might lie ahead when the time came for him sorrowfully to break the news that their fake engagement had bitten the dust.

She would definitely have to move to London, close by where he could keep an eye on her, but how easy was it going to be to take her away from familiar surroundings?

He would also, while in the process of recovering from a broken engagement, have to rustle up some enthusiasm for the whole prospect of finding someone else with whom to tie the knot.

Except, for some reason, the thought of that as yet unknown woman filled him with a certain distaste.

He had worked out what this woman would be like, not in great detail but as a rough sketch, but now that he had found himself discovering complex sides to his PA's personality he was beginning to revise the one-dimensional cardboard parameters he had had in place. He also knew that whoever he ended up with would have to be sharp, would have to be someone who got him and who understood his sense of humour.

An image of Abby flashed through his head and he frowned. Anyone who had high expectations of romantic love and everything that entailed would definitely be out. Lucy had been a vital learning curve when it came to that.

Absorbed in a bout of unusual introspection, he neither heard nor noticed Abby as she paused at the top of the short flight of stairs to look down at him as he stood, still frowning, by the front door.

They were going to one the fancy restaurants he had mentioned earlier. When he had announced this, she had immediately countered with the perfectly logical suggestion that they should use the evening to meet some of the clients whom they'd arranged to see before they'd left London, considering his grandmother had decided not to join them, and initially he had agreed.

He felt, rather than heard, her presence and looked up. Then looked again, then found that *all* he seemed capable of doing was looking.

Her hair was loose, silky, straight and falling just past her shoulders in a shiny sweep. Her eyes looked different, smoky and sultry, and the shiny gloss of her lipstick emphasised the soft fullness of her mouth.

But it was the transformation of her figure that really captured his attention and held it.

The dress was short, revealing long, slim, shapely legs. There was nothing revealing about it, because it was a simple shift, but somehow the pale turquoise silk hit all the right curves in all the right places so that the eye was drawn to the swell of small breasts and the dip of a narrow waist.

She tucked some hair behind one ear as she walked towards him and he noticed that she was wearing big hoop earrings, which was vaguely shocking, because he'd never thought of her as the big hoop-earring type.

'Are you okay?' Abby asked politely, standing in

front of him, quietly pleased at the expression on his face, because he was a guy who was way too casual when it came to beautiful women. She knew she was no beauty, especially compared to the women usually to be found hanging onto his arm, but he'd only ever seen her in working clothes or jeans and trainers since she had been here, and the change obviously stunned him. Good! 'You look as though you've seen a ghost.'

Gabriel quickly found his voice. 'Slight change of plans. I've rearranged several of the meetings for London and I have managed to touch base with the CEO of the electronics company,' he announced, watching Abby closely. 'I can follow up on that conversation by email. Both companies are keen for a deal, so I don't anticipate any lost opportunities because our original schedule has had to be changed.'

'What? I honestly don't feel as though I'm doing what I'm being paid to do,' she protested.

'You're obeying the boss's orders,' Gabriel said silkily. 'What's there to complain about? Enjoy the change of pace.'

It irked him to realise that she baulked at accepting what any other woman would have grabbed with both hands outstretched. Maybe, he thought, he'd grown accustomed to excessive female gratitude when in receipt of his attention and his lavish gifts.

Abby was more than a bit annoyed. With next to no notice, he had informed her that the clients they had arranged to meet had cancelled! At this point, hair washed and with Ava hovering to see them off, Abby had no option but to stick to the 'fancy restaurant' plan, which now felt like a date and not like a safe business event with manageable parameters.

Gabriel gathered himself, disconcerted to have been thrown by Abby's appearance. 'Right. We should go.' He spun round and preceded her to the door.

'I hope I look okay, even though there won't be any client to impress,' something mischievous in her prompted Abby to say, and she gave him a disingenuously anxious look from under her sooty lashes.

Their eyes met and she regretted that mischievous impulse when he smiled at her slowly. 'Fishing? I didn't think you were the sort...'

'Of course I wasn't fishing!' she protested, standing back and fiddling with the strap of her shoulder bag, which was the only thing about her outfit that hadn't been bought three hours previously. 'I just hoped, er, that where we're going...that I'm dressed appropriately for wherever we happen to be going. I... I don't have a great deal of experience when it comes to eating out in fancy restaurants.' Under normal circumstances, going to a restaurant to entertain a client with him would have had her reaching for something sober and, yes, grey, but with Ava around and the family heirloom on her finger she'd gone for...the right outfit for the part she was playing.

'Sexy,' he purred, back to his usual self. He lounged against the doorframe, shoved his hand in his trouser pocket and stared down at her.

Skewered by those deep, dark eyes, Abby shifted her gaze, but he filled her line of vision. Had he just called her *sexy*? *Her*?

When it came to sexy, *he* was the one who fitted the description! In a simple white shirt with sleeves rolled to the elbows and a pair of dark trousers, he was the epitome of exotic, elegant, casual *cool*.

'Thank you very much, although there's no need for the compliment, considering your grandmother isn't around.'

'Accept it for what it is,' Gabriel murmured. 'There's nothing more unattractive than a woman who snaps when a guy pays her a compliment.'

Abby bristled and he burst out laughing. 'Right about now, you can start telling me what a dinosaur I am, but in the meantime let's get to the restaurant. We're running behind time and I wouldn't want the manager of the place to give our table to someone else.'

'I doubt he'd dare.' Thankfully her breathing had returned to normal.

Gabriel dealt her a slashing sideways smile. 'You have a point.

Never mix work and pleasure. Gabriel spent the evening reminding himself of the thousands of ways his libido could ambush his common sense, but he still caught himself staring at her doing the most mundane of things: reading the menu…turning to smile at the waiter as he took the order…playing with the stem of her wine glass and then half-closing her eyes as she took the first sip…

He also noticed all those covert glances other men gave her. When she sashayed her way to the ladies' just before they were ready to leave, he could swear tongues were hanging from mouths, and never before had he found such overt displays of attraction so repulsive.

Especially when you considered that the majority of the men there had said goodbye to their forties a while back and were sitting opposite women who presumably were their wives!

They made the trip back to the villa in record time.

It had been a long meal, a taster menu that had continued for over two hours, and the lights in the villa were out by the time Gabriel inserted the key into the front door and pushed it open.

She brushed past him and even that vague passing physical contact made him ache.

'Enjoyed the evening, I hope?' he asked gruffly, moving out of harm's way and wondering when he had suddenly turned into a horny adolescent, and why. 'In spite of there being no clients at the table to keep us busy?'

Abby smiled. She'd loved every second of it. She'd loved the food, the ambience, the glorious old elegance of the restaurant. She'd loved the choice of wine, the strength of the coffee, the novelty of the *amuse-bouche*...

She'd loved his company.

He'd been amusing, witty and charming, and all of that had gone to her head faster than the several glasses of wine she had drunk, barely aware of her glass being topped up the minute it looked as though it might need a refill.

He'd stopped being her boss. Even on night one, when she had lain on that bed, frozen like a statue while he'd worked next to her, he'd been her boss. And the following night she hadn't seen him at all, because he'd worked until late and then risen before she'd opened her eyes in the morning. Through all those deliberate touches for the sake of his grandmother, she hadn't forgotten that they were playing a game and that reality awaited them when they were back in London and she donned her neat little suit and pumps and sat down in front of him to go through work for the day.

But tonight…

It had started when she had walked into that boutique and abandoned herself to doing something she had never given much thought to—shopping.

Then later, when she had stood in front of him and *smelled* the scent of attraction, *sensed* that he was seeing her, maybe for the first time, as a *woman* and not his efficient PA, something had changed in her.

She'd stopped being the well-behaved, neat, tidy woman who sorted his life out for him, did her job and worked overtime without complaining.

She'd been herself, and had allowed herself to open up and respond as though they were two people just out having a good time.

It was dangerous.

And it was dangerous how much she knew him, how easy it was to be lulled by his sexy, seductive banter. Who even knew whether he was deliberately flirting? Who could tell whether it had meant anything when he'd looked at her for just a bit too long with those lazy, dark eyes as he'd relaxed back in his chair and sipped from his glass of wine?

'It was wonderful. The restaurant is to die for and the food was heavenly. Your grandmother is very lucky to have something of that standard just round the corner.'

Gabriel raked his fingers through his hair and half-turned away. She looked so damned glorious that he wanted to step forward, yank her towards him, kiss her senseless, then take her up to the bedroom and do all sorts of other things to her that would leave her even more senseless.

He'd been plagued with uncomfortable arousal for the duration of the evening, and he knew that if he carried on looking at her now and letting his imagination run riot he wouldn't be the only one to notice his excitement. It would be evident to her as well.

'Not sure she makes a habit of going to five-star restaurants. Her diet has been, through necessity, a simple one.'

Silence. And this time the king of silence was finding it hard to deal with—although she, it had to be said, was as controlled as he was restless. The shoe was most firmly on the other foot.

'Think I'll get some work in,' he said abruptly, spinning round on his heels and heading in the direction of the office at the end of the long villa.

Left alone, Abby felt a shard of disappointment pierce her, and she fiercely reminded herself that whilst *she* might have let pretend-world merge with real world *he* obviously had a lot more control.

'Good idea!' she said brightly, moving off in the opposite direction towards the staircase.

'Don't wait up.' Safer to sleep in the office, he thought, even if it meant a dodgy back the next day. 'I might do an all-nighter.'

Abby laughed and squashed the thought that an empty bed was the most unappealing thing in the world, especially after one of the best evenings of her life. She turned round and threw over her shoulder without looking at him, 'Wouldn't dream of it.'

CHAPTER SEVEN

GABRIEL LOOKED AT his watch. He hadn't thought it possible for time to move as slowly as it had. He'd been cooped up in the office for the past two hours and it had felt like a lifetime.

Was he going to sleep there? Not a chance. One look at the sleeping options had put paid to any such plan. Besides, he'd managed to spend the past two nights sharing a bed with her. She'd stuck to her side, as though glued to the space, and he'd had his usual brief sleep, waking while she was enjoying her first dream and heading downstairs for strong coffee and a backlog of emails.

Touching hadn't been on his mind. He'd reined in any hint of his imagination getting frisky and had told himself that there was no way he was going to jeopardise his professional relationship with her by making a pass.

Even though the combination of him, a bed and a sexy woman didn't bear thinking about.

But tonight…

Something had been different, a little shift that had made his blood run hot.

He got up and flexed, stretching out the stiffness of having been sitting for two hours. When he looked at his watch, it was to find that it was after one in the morning, and he was pretty sure she would be sound asleep. For someone who had been as skittish as a colt about sharing a bed with him, she'd managed to fall asleep for the past two nights with no problem at all.

Still in the clothes he had worn to go to the restaurant, Gabriel began heading up the stairs, making sure not to switch on any lights.

His movements were as stealthy as a panther. By the time he was standing outside the bedroom, he had unbuttoned his shirt and tugged it out of the waistband of his trousers.

She had left the door slightly ajar, as she had the night before, and he had easily read the motive behind that. *Don't wake me,* that gesture had shrieked. There was no way she would find it comfortable to be awake when he slipped under the sheets. He grinned at the thought of her blushing discomfort, but then sobered up when he realised that *he* would find it all slightly awkward as well, even though he was an expert when it came to all things between the sheets.

Indeed, he had spent at least one night sleeping next to a woman with whom he had had no intention of making love but with whom, for reasons beyond his control, he had found himself sharing a bed. She had come onto him with the clumsy determination of someone who'd had just a tiny bit too much to drink, and he had had no problem gently swatting away her advances until she had nodded off into snoring slumber. He could have been sleeping next to a mannequin for all the temptation he had felt to touch.

He pushed open the door very gently and shut it just as gently behind him. He heard the soft click and then, reassured by Abby's even breathing, Gabriel padded towards the bathroom, stripping off his shirt en route and tossing it onto the floor.

Abby didn't move a muscle. Wasn't he supposed to be sleeping in the office? Doing an all-nighter? She would never have dreamt of reading her book for an hour if she'd known that—she would have been on red alert to fall asleep and *be* asleep in record-breaking time because he was returning to the bedroom!

It was dark in the room, but not so dark that she hadn't seen the ripple of muscled torso as he'd begun removing his shirt.

Abby felt wired. She wanted to keep still but suddenly had to move because she was beginning to get pins and needles in her feet.

She moved just as Gabriel exited the bathroom, the light behind him throwing his body into shadow. His torso was bare. Was that how he had slept next to her for the past two nights? Had she been sharing the bed with a half-naked Gabriel? Thankfully he was in a pair of loose drawstring bottoms which were slung low on his hips and looked ridiculously sexy.

'Did I wake you?' Gabriel reached to turn off the bathroom light and the bedroom was plunged into immediate darkness, but then within seconds his eyes acclimatised because the moon was managing to seep through the shutters, casting just enough of a dim light to outline the dark shapes in the room.

Abby didn't say anything because her tongue was suddenly glued to the roof of her mouth.

'I thought,' Gabriel said conversationally as he strolled towards the bed, sending her nervous system into panicked overdrive, 'You would have been asleep by now.' He slipped under the covers and propped himself up on his side to look at her.

'Are you finished working already?' Abby wondered how likely it was that she could introduce some kind of work-related issues into whatever brief, embarrassing conversation she would have to have with the wretched man who looked infuriatingly bright-eyed and bushy-tailed from what she could make out in the darkness.

'It's after one. I might not need much sleep, Abby, but an entire night without any would test even me.'

'I thought you mentioned that you might be sleeping in the office.'

'Is that why you're still awake?'

'Of course not!'

'Oh, good. Because, were that to be the case, then I would have to question your assertion that you could share a bed naked with me and not notice my presence.'

'I never said that.'

The conversation was being conducted in hushed whispers and that made Abby feel as though they were being naughty kids indulging in something that would get them into trouble should they get caught. She cleared her throat and frantically tried to think of a good way to end the conversation, because her whole body was on fire.

In between the self-indulgent buying of designer clothes, she'd somehow contrived to forget that she meant to buy a set of drab pyjamas. Probably because such an item hadn't been stocked in any of the boutiques she'd entered. Rich women who wore silk and cashmere obviously didn't do flannelette as well.

'My mistake,' Gabriel murmured. He shifted. Thought about that glimpse of the very sexy night gown he had glimpsed on the single passing occasion.

'Well...' Abby faked a yawn. 'I should get some sleep. Busy day tomorrow if we plan on touching base with the CEO of Mira Holdings.'

'No plans there.'

'But I thought...'

'I know. However, as you can surmise by now, all plans are in a state of flux. I don't want my grandmother suspecting that this is anything but the real deal, and as a guy who is supposedly newly loved up, rushing off clutching a briefcase with a row of pens in my top pocket isn't going to cut it. I'm keeping on top of things in London, getting through essential emails, and I've done what I can do about the deals I had lined up to work on over here—but that's about as far as I can go for the rest of the time we're here.'

'You grandmother obviously doesn't know you,' Abby couldn't resist saying in a tart undertone. 'If she thinks that you would actually take time off to relax when there's work to be done.'

'Maybe she thinks I would if I were loved up enough.'

'And would you?'

'Never been there, so couldn't tell you.'

'I should get some sleep.'

'You looked beautiful tonight.'

Abby's breath caught in her throat and her eyes widened. She clamped her thighs tightly together but she could feel the dampness between her legs and the push of her nipples against her soft, silky nightie. With every pore in her being, she was aware of just how scantily dressed she was under the protection of the cover.

'Don't say that,' she whispered.

'It's the truth,' Gabriel said huskily. This was playing with fire, and he had promised himself that it was something he wouldn't do, but something was pulling him towards the fire and he wanted to plunge his hands in just to see how it would feel. 'Don't tell me you didn't notice all those men looking at you.'

'I don't notice stuff like that,' Abby squeaked. 'It was probably the dress.'

'You're running yourself down. That creep really did a number on you, Abby. Is that why you hide behind those drab clothes?'

'I don't hide behind drab clothes!' But she giggled, because he was just so predictable in certain ways. 'I come to work, Gabriel. I'm not going to wear thigh-high boots and micro-minis!'

'Shame. It would be interesting to see how you would look in that get-up.'

'I'm going to sleep now.'

'How easy are you going to find that?'

'Sorry?'

'You want to keep the walls up between us, but they've been coming down, haven't they?'

'No!'

'It's understandable, when you think about it.' Gabriel overrode her protesting squeak. He wanted to touch her. She was so close, all tucked up in the sheets like a mummy. The overhead fan was on, a soft purring sound that was curiously restful, but she'd be hot under those covers. As hot as he was. Hot, hard and turned on by playing with fire.

'I'm not interested in thinking about it.' But, that said, she was still looking at him, mesmerised by his dark beauty and the seductive journey of his words, leading her down all sorts of taboo routes.

'I mean,' he mused, reaching to trail one finger across her cheek, 'One minute you're my perfect PA, and the next minute we're engaged.'

Abby barely took in the ironic, tongue-in-cheek wickedness of his observation because that finger on her cheek was devastating. She couldn't breathe, couldn't blink. She heard herself sigh, an unthinkably telling sound that penetrated the silence of the room and shattered the illusion that she was in control of the situation.

'We're not engaged,' she managed to croak and Gabriel smiled. She saw the flash of white.

'No,' he agreed softly, 'We're not. But tell me that we're not in thrall to the same feeling.'

'I don't know what you mean.'

'And have you asked yourself this…?' He trailed his finger along her neck and noted the way she shifted, arching a little and half-closing her eyes. It was an instinctive reaction and it said a lot. 'We could go there.'

Had she asked herself that? No! Had she wondered what it would be like to touch him, make love with him? Yes! And not just now, not just in the past few days. She'd thought about it in that hazy window between wake and sleep. Thought about those strong, brown hands roving over her body and touching her.

'We couldn't…no…we definitely shouldn't…'

Gabriel smiled again, a slow, curling smile. 'Maybe we shouldn't,' he conceded, 'But we most certainly could.'

'I… Gabriel, I'm not the kind of girl who indulges in one-night stands.'

'And I'm not the kind of man who has ever mixed

business with pleasure.' He paused and his eyes dipped to her full mouth. 'Are you sure you're not a one-night stand girl?' he murmured, more because he wanted to give breath to his curiosity than because he didn't believe her.

'I've never done that in my life before. Never even thought about it.'

'Never thought about it? Sure about that? Not even when you were in that club?'

Abby reddened. 'Do you ever forget anything?' she asked. His finger was still brushing her skin and she was loving it.

'A long memory is the secret of my success. And you haven't answered my question.' He felt an amusing spurt of jealousy, and not just at the thought of her flirting with some guy but talking to him, opening up to him, sharing confidences with him. Had she done that?

'I wasn't interested in a one-night stand,' Abby admitted. 'I was interested in a possible relationship, but unfortunately...'

'So where do we go from here?' Gabriel traced the swell of her breast and she shuddered. 'Admittedly this is no relationship, but neither is it a one-night stand. We're here for another five nights.'

'Gabriel...'

'I want you,' he told her bluntly. 'Trust me, I see the pitfalls, but hell, once we both know the nature of the road we're walking down then where's the danger?'

'You make it sound so easy.' Abby could scarcely believe that she was having this conversation because it went against every single thing she believed in. A one-night stand? Or, as he put it, a *five-night* stand...?

But where had being sensible got her? One date since

Jason and that had been a disaster. She hadn't even fancied him! She'd been so busy ticking boxes that she had forgotten that there was one very important box that had to be ticked—the sexual attraction box.

Gabriel didn't tick any boxes *but* the sexual attraction one. She should be running a mile from this situation. She had given herself long lectures on the importance of avoiding anything like this, yet here she was, with his finger touching her oh, so lightly and setting sparks off in parts of her she'd never known existed.

Temptation kicked in hard and fast. She *knew* the score. She probably knew the score better than anyone else because she'd seen him in action, had witnessed the ease with which he moved from woman to woman—had even clocked the way he had reacted to his broken engagement. He didn't do relationships. He didn't do commitment. He did sex. One day he would get married but the marriage, as he had pointed out, would be an arrangement that suited both parties involved. There was no room in his life for love. Oh, yes, she knew the score all right.

'It's only hard when wires get crossed,' Gabriel murmured. This touching business was driving him insane. He honestly had no idea what he would do if she gave the matter some thought and decided against it. He'd never had to take so much time before and it was agony.

'There's no chance of crossed wires,' Abby murmured unsteadily.

'No, we're on the same page. We may not be in Las Vegas, but what happens here stays here. Then we go back to London and we return to reality. It's as easy as that. But, if you have any doubts, then I'll respect that and you won't have to fear that I'll make a nuisance of myself.'

'I know you'd never do that.'

'I'd even take the floor.'

'No, you wouldn't,' she said wryly and Gabriel burst out laughing.

'See?' he teased huskily. 'You know me better than anyone. We go into this with our eyes wide open and, trust me, I'll take you places you've never even dreamed about.'

'You're so arrogant, Gabriel.'

He didn't answer. Instead, he cut off anything else she might have been thinking of saying. He was fed up with chat.

Abby was pressed back as his mouth hit hers in a hungry, greedy, demanding kiss that took her breath away. She clasped his shoulders, digging her short nails into his skin and rearing up to meet his devouring kiss. Tongue melded with tongue and, as he kissed her, he dispensed with the cocoon of sheets and blankets in which she had encased herself.

Abby was aware of bed linen slipping off the bed, being kicked to the side as he positioned himself over her, straddling her without removing his mouth from hers.

Wild with desire, she opened her legs, wrapped them around his thighs and groaned into his mouth when she felt the rock-hard bulge of his desire. Every forbidden fantasy, all those fantasies she hadn't admitted even to herself, exploded in a burst of desire that brought a surge of heat between her legs. She squirmed against him, and he reared up and looked down at her.

She was beautiful. Exquisite. Not in the obvious, 'if

you've got it, flaunt it' kind of way of the women he had dated in the past, and not in the rake-thin, all legs and jutting cheekbones way that Lucy had had. She was slender, soft and irresistible in the way she looked at him, wide eyed and wanting, but trying to resist being obvious about it.

The sexy little nightgown was every which way and he hooked his fingers at the hem and gently tugged it up. As soon as it was over her head, she folded her arms across her breasts and looked to one side, blushing furiously and breathing hard.

Very gently he unfolded her arms and pinned them to her sides. He had to close his eyes and breathe in deeply because the impact of those naked breasts on him was like nothing he had felt before.

Stunning.

Her breasts were small, round and pert, with nipples that were big for the size of them and very well-defined.

He linked his fingers through hers, spread her arms wide and lowered himself to her breasts.

The ache in his groin was suffocating. He wanted to take her, forget about the foreplay, but he wasn't going to do that because something in him was propelling him to take his time, to be gentle, to give her the space truly to open up to him.

He nuzzled the soft, pale orbs, latched onto one pulsing nipple and suckled, drawing it into his mouth, enjoying the way she moved, sighed and writhed underneath him. He drew back and then devoted time to her other nipple, nuzzling and taking his time, and only finally releasing one hand so that he could play with her between her legs, feel her wetness through the sexy knickers and then, sliding his hand underneath them, through the skimpy underwear.

Abby gasped. She was bombarded by racing sensations in every part of her body. She felt faint when she glanced down to see his dark head at her breast.

He looked up, caught her eye and moved to cover her mouth with his. Touching him was a journey of discovery, a forbidden journey, and her fingers trembled as she traced the back of his neck and then the muscular cords of his shoulder blades as he continued to kiss her.

'You surprised me with your choice of underwear...' he broke apart to say.

Abby blushed. 'Did you think I might wear granny knickers?'

'Your choice of work gear doesn't advertise someone wild and daring underneath.'

'You're accustomed to women who let it all hang out.'

'More fool me. I'm finding that I like the element of surprise. Silk and lace...nice...erotic. Do I make you feel erotic?'

'Gabriel!'

'I've always liked the way my name sounds on your lips,' he murmured, nipping her ear gently. 'When you say *Gabriel*, all sorts of enticing images enter my head. Throw in the unexpected nightwear, and I'm an engine revving to hit the tracks.'

'The nightwear's only unexpected because it's on me and you've never got past thinking of me as someone whose dress code is all about looking right for an office. There have been times when I've smiled thinking of what you were looking at on the outside and what was underneath.'

'Well, well, well… The things we discover about one another… I'd never have guessed…'

'I haven't discovered anything about you,' Abby said on a hitched breath as his exploring hand found her damp crotch and began massaging her through the lacy material, which she had yet to remove.

'That's because you know everything there is to know already.' He slipped his hand under the lace and stroked gently, rhythmically, until she was moaning and breathing fast.

Her thoughts became tangled. He was touching her, making her body sing, and right here, right now, he was no longer her boss and she was no longer his PA. He was a man, she was a woman and they were wildly attracted to one another. Abby had never thought about the power of lust because she had always assumed that it was just a sort of bonus with the bigger player, which was love. She had thought that she loved Jason. In retrospect, she had drifted into something that had felt comfortable, and had been more in love with the feeling of being in love than anything else.

Jason had held no surprises.

This man was all surprise. He was also teaching her what it felt like to be at the mercy of her body.

There was no common sense left in her when he touched her the way he was touching her now, sliding his fingers into her, teasing her until she wanted to scream.

She clung like a limpet, twisting and turning as he stroked and sent her pulses soaring into the stratosphere.

When he broke apart, she felt bereft.

'Needs must,' he said, sliding his legs over the side

of the bed and standing up to reach for his wallet, which had hit the floor along with his trousers.

Abby could detect the unusually husky undertone, and she knew that he was as out of control as she was, although he was a lot better at camouflaging it.

That afforded her a surge of heady pleasure that this man, who could have any woman he wanted, might go weak for *her*.

She looked at him from under lowered lashes and her breath caught in her throat as he began removing the loose, cotton bottoms she assumed he had donned for the sake of decency.

He retrieved a condom from the wallet. She knew that without having actually seen him do it.

She was holding her breath and she exhaled very, very slowly as he was revealed to her in all his glory.

She sat up as he sauntered to the side of the bed and, before he could slide in to join her, she took him in her hands, caressed his impressive girth and then took him into her mouth and began sucking.

Her own daring shocked her. She stroked him with her tongue and felt his unsteadiness when he plunged his hand into her hair and guided her movements, his feet squarely planted, his breathing as raspy as hers.

'That feels so bloody good,' Gabriel said in a driven, strangled undertone. He'd died and gone to heaven. He could barely comprehend the level of pleasure she was giving him and, for the first time in his life, he knew that reluctantly he'd have to stop her from doing what she was doing or else it would be over between them all too soon.

He eased her off him and took a few moments to rescue some of his self-control, then he was in the bed with her before she could wreak more devastation.

'You're a witch,' he growled, covering her body with his and kissing her until she was bucking and pulling him hard against her.

He wanted to take his time but his need to be sated was pulling him in a different direction. He wanted to be *in her*, thrusting and feeling her tightness around him.

Instead, he controlled the impulse, even though it took almost more will power than he had at his command.

He explored her body with his mouth. He returned to her breasts and lost himself in their soft perfection. He teased her stiffened nipple with the tip of his tongue and then suckled it until she was writhing under him.

He placed his big hand on her hip and then slid it along her thigh, all the while easing himself down her body, his mouth never breaking contact with her skin.

He luxuriated in the salty taste of her body. She was perspiring, just as he was, as hot as he was. He circled her belly button with his tongue and then moved lower, amused when she tried to snap shut her legs.

'Gabriel!' Abby squeaked breathlessly, and he raised his eyes to her and grinned.

'Yes?' he queried innocently. 'Instructions? I don't need any. I can find my way down all by myself…'

'Somehow, this feels wicked.'

'Naughty but nice? It's going to be a whole lot better than nice. Trust me on that, *cara*. Once I start, you're not going to want me to stop.'

And strangely, even though part of her brain was saying otherwise, she did trust him. She abandoned herself to an experience that felt shockingly and thrillingly intimate.

He settled between her legs and began to taste her with his tongue, licking, probing and teasing, and she groaned softly, wriggled and groaned again. She reached down and curled her fingers into his hair and, God, he was so right: she didn't want him to stop because it felt so good.

Her legs fell apart then she wrapped them around him and arched a little as he reached underneath her, pushing her up against his questing mouth.

She sucked in her breath and didn't release it as her body began ascending to its orgasm.

'No,' she managed to croak, by which she meant, *I want you inside me...*

If she hadn't been as weak as a kitten, helpless in the face of this deluge of physical sensation, she might have done a little more than just moan and whimper as her movements under him became more frantic. And then she was toppling over the edge, crying out as she climaxed in long, shuddering spasms against his mouth.

'Not fair,' she managed to gasp as he drew up so that he was once more kissing her. She could taste herself on his mouth. If felt wildly, wildly decadent.

'Don't worry.' Gabriel heaved himself up on both arms only to bend so that he could nuzzle the slender curve of her neck. 'We're not nearly finished yet.'

He wasn't lying. He had stamina and he was intent on pleasuring her.

He was a considerate lover, barely thinking about himself as he stroked and teased her body back to a place where she was hot for him all over again, and this time he didn't take her over the edge. This time, he reached for the protection he had flung onto the bedside table and levered himself up so that he could carefully roll it on.

Abby could barely contain her excitement as he entered her, slowly at first, stretching her because he was so big, but their bodies couldn't have been more fashioned for one another. Her wetness embraced him and, as he thrust deeper and harder into her, a whole new world of physical satisfaction opened up.

She couldn't get enough and she urged him on, her body gradually moving in perfect tempo with his until they were as one.

She felt him climax just as she felt herself come undone once again. She cried out, arching against him, her small breasts pushing up, her whole body bathed in perspiration.

Her orgasm seemed to go on for ever, until finally she was utterly and totally spent and she sagged like a rag doll, eyes closed, cheeks flushed.

She was aware of him easing himself off her. She could have slept for England. Gabriel, meanwhile, left the bedroom and acute disappointment seized her when she thought that he might have vanished off to change so that he could go downstairs and resume work. He didn't strike her as the sort who enjoyed pillow talk, but she would have loved to talk, talk and talk, if only she weren't so sleepy.

Abby kept her eyes shut and reminded herself that this was a little fling and it was all about the sex. Lord knew, if the situation hadn't been what it was, they would never have ended up in bed together.

Tender gestures and intimate conversation wouldn't feature highly on the agenda.

She knew that he'd left the bathroom, but rather than

witness his disappearing act she kept her eyes closed. They flew open fast enough when she felt herself being picked up as though she weighed nothing.

'Don't think you're going to fall asleep on me,' he chuckled, walking with her to the bathroom and nudging the door open with his foot.

'What are you doing?'

'I'm going to give you a bath.'

Abby looked at him and laughed. She dropped a kiss briefly on his mouth and fought down the dangerous thought that this was just perfect.

'I thought you were getting changed and then heading downstairs to get some work done,' she confessed, eyes popping when she saw the luxurious bubble bath he had run for her.

'You won't be getting rid of me quite so easily.' Gabriel lowered her into the water as gently as if she were a piece of china, and then he stood back to contemplate his handiwork with satisfaction before getting in to join her. 'We're engaged…remember? There's nothing more I want to do than have you glued to my side.'

And then what? Abby thought distractedly, because he was manoeuvring her so that she had her back to him and he could begin soaping her. *What,* she thought, *happens then?*

CHAPTER EIGHT

SPRAWLED OUT ON one of the chairs by the pool, it struck Gabriel that he hadn't actually done this since his grandmother had moved to the villa years ago. He'd visited, he'd eaten meals in the kitchen served by his grandmother's daily housekeeper, he'd taken her out on countless occasions—but he'd never sat by the pool in a pair of swimming trunks, relaxing.

In his world, relaxing usually involved women, and sex was always on the menu. And, relaxing though that situation was, it was too much like a carefully crafted game to be completely relaxing.

There was a woman now. Sex was most definitely on the menu. In fact, just thinking about her was rousing a libido that had been on red alert ever since he and Abby had decided to turn their fake relationship into something rather more substantial.

Gabriel grinned and shifted, already looking forward to getting into bed with her later.

But this didn't feel like the usual carefully crafted game. Which was why he could sit here, without a computer in sight and with his mobile phone in the bedroom, and kick back.

It felt good. Novel. He was doing what millions of

people did and took for granted when they went on holiday, yet for him it felt like he was exploring a brave, new world.

He shifted and watched as Abby dove into the pool. She was a graceful swimmer and, unlike the sort of women he was accustomed to dating—unlike even Lucy, who had not been anything like the women he was accustomed to dating—Abby actually didn't mind getting her hair wet. Lying and tanning seemed to hold little interest for her.

She was sporty, he had discovered. She enjoyed hiking. In the idyllic, rural bubble in which she had been raised, she had surfed, gone camping and explored the countryside by bike. He had pieced together a picture of someone whose life had followed a pleasant if predictable path, culminating in her engagement to the guy who had ditched her when big city life had begun to weave its spell.

She'd toughened up, built a shell around herself and taken refuge in her privacy, but underneath the walls there was a completely different woman.

He wondered what it might be like to go on a proper holiday with her, one that hadn't stemmed from unusual circumstances, and he frowned, because it was the last sort of idle speculation he should be indulging.

'You're not thinking about work, are you?'

Gabriel sat forward, arms draped over his thighs, and stared at the bikini-clad figure of his so-called fiancée who was peering at him from the pool, hair plastered around a face bare of any make-up. She was one hundred percent natural and, if he closed his eyes, he could almost smell her clean, floral scent, the one that filled his nostrils and made him want to make love to her over and over again.

'Really want to know what I'm thinking about?' he drawled, vaulting upright and strolling towards her.

Abby's eyes darkened and she laughed, because she could read the intent in his eyes and it fired up something in her, something that made her want to leap out of the swimming pool and drag him off to the nearest empty room so that she could have her wicked way with him.

'Are you thinking that the pool looks really inviting and you'd like nothing better than to join me?'

'I can certainly think of nothing better than joining you,' Gabriel agreed. 'But it's only…' he glanced at his watch '…five-thirty, which means I have to endure a few more hours before I can get you where I want you.'

'You shouldn't be wishing away your time here,' Abby chided, but she was still laughing as he slid into the water and kissed her briefly on the mouth, before ducking under and surfacing to shake his head like a dog shaking off water. 'You should be hoping it passes slowly, all the better to enjoy your grandmother's company. She's just so thrilled to have you here. I can't believe she's actually given her housekeeper the rest of the week off so that she can cook all your favourite meals.' Abby swivelled so that she was backed against the side of the pool, elbows supporting her, treading water as she looked at him. 'It's no wonder you're so spoiled.'

'I admit I don't have a problem when it comes to getting my own way.' He knew that his grandmother was resting. She'd actually made it to the pool and had swum a few laps, encouraged by Abby, but that burst of activity had taken it out of her and she had retired half an hour ago to have a lie down.

With that in mind, Gabriel caged Abby in, his muscular arms on either side of hers, and he kissed her, a long, drugging kiss that barely allowed her to come up for air. Keeping his eyes on the house, he casually reached down and cupped her between her legs.

'I like the bikini, by the way. Good choice, although I have to say that if my grandmother wasn't here I would consign it to the wardrobe and forbid you from coming into the swimming pool with anything on.'

'Very chauvinistic,' Abby said on a breathless whimper, as the hand cupping her began to work its way underneath the bikini bottom. He'd somehow managed to persuade her that anything remotely constricting as a bra was a disposable item of clothing, and her skin burned whenever she thought of him coming up from behind and slipping his hand underneath her top so that he could play with her breasts.

'I'm a dinosaur,' Gabriel agreed without batting an eye. 'I like my women hot and ready for me. Like now. You're wet, and it has nothing to do with the fact that we're both in a swimming pool. Like me to make you even wetter?'

'Gabriel.' Abby breathed brokenly as he began to tease her with his expert touch. 'This is not the time… oh, oh, Gabriel…or the place… Your grandmother… Oh, that feels so good…'

'She's sound asleep and this is just the right time and place for me to pleasure my woman.' With one hand, he cupped the back of her neck so that he could kiss her, while he busied himself with his other hand, his fingers sliding up and down, gathering a rhythm that built and built and built until she was whimpering and moaning.

She gave a spasm against his hand and cried out as the orgasm peaked, taking her breath away and then gradually subsiding, leaving her limp as a rag doll for a few seconds. Then she slowly opened her eyes and looked at him, dazed.

'I can't believe you just did that.' She breathed unsteadily and Gabriel grinned and kissed her, but this time a quick dip on her mouth.

'I get a kick out of taking you places you haven't been before. I like it.'

'I wish I could do the same for you,' Abby said fervently.

'You do. I'm here, aren't I? In a swimming pool, playing truant from work.'

'You must have done that before, when you've gone on holiday with whatever buxom brunette you happened to be going out with.'

'To tell you the truth, I haven't taken many women on holiday. Anywhere.'

'Why not?'

Gabriel shrugged. He knew why—because a holiday would have felt like a level of commitment and one that held no interest for him. Always on guard against any woman wanting more than he was prepared to give, he had developed a keen instinct for staying away from situations that could become complicated. Cosy holidays came into that category.

'Naturally, there have been one or two brief weekends abroad. They usually involved expensive shopping or expensive skiing in a crowd. Do you ski?'

Abby laughed. 'I don't like shopping and I don't ski.'

'I'm surprised, given how active your childhood was.'

'My parents weren't exactly rolling in money, Gabriel. They had enough for the things that mattered but definitely not enough to throw around on skiing holidays. My dad was always careful with money which is why…you know…'

'I get it. Why the injection of cash you'll be getting for this little escapade will be invaluable for him.' Gabriel frowned, because for a minute there he really hadn't liked being reminded that she was doing this for a reason, and that this pleasant little situation was all part and parcel of a business transaction.

'You're good for Ava, you know.' He changed the subject. 'She likes you. Feels relaxed around you. That's something I honestly didn't give a great deal of thought to when we began this charade.'

Abby didn't say anything. Being reminded that what they had wasn't real felt like a bucket of cold water being poured over her head, and that alarmed her, because the reality of this situation was not something she could afford to forget. Not for a second.

'No, well…' She shrugged. 'Women tend to bond with women, and you know you can be a little daunting.'

'Daunting,' Gabriel mused. 'Is that a compliment, I wonder?'

'It's true. I've spent a lot more time with Ava than I thought I would, and she's in awe of her brilliant, charismatic grandson. You have to remember that you have that effect on people.'

'Although not on you. Or maybe I'm wrong. Are you in awe of me?'

'No,' Abby said truthfully. 'I'm not.'

'It's going to be tough when she has to be told that

you and I are over.' It was good that reminders were dropped that this was an artificial situation and one that had a very strict timeline.

'But, in due course, she'll meet the woman you really intend to marry and she'll get along with whoever you choose just as well—probably better, because at least she'll be able to really look forward to wedding bells and great-grandchildren.' Something caught in her throat and she looked away. 'Poor Ava keeps trying to coerce me into talking about wedding dresses and setting a date. She must wonder why I'm not more excited about the big day.'

Did he detect something in her voice? He remembered that she had been ditched by her fiancé. Of course, this would be hard for her, but he wasn't going to get wrapped up in any long conversations about that. 'It'll become apparent when this is all over.' He kissed her neck, tilting her head back, but for once Abby wasn't distracted by her body and its responses.

'How can you be so detached?' She breathed, and she could have kicked herself when he stilled and drew back to look at her levelly, his dark eyes cool and assessing.

'How do you imagine I should be reacting, Abby?'

'I guess a little more emotionally, because she *is* your grandmother, and I know you love her very much.'

It was a passing statement, and it was fact, but suddenly Gabriel detected the sound of alarm bells because the way she'd said it, the easy acceptance of knowing him in a way that was bone-deep...

'I'm detached because I haven't lost sight of the ball,' he said abruptly, shoving aside the unsettling suspicion that he had, a couple of times. 'I've never seen my grandmother this energised, and I'm very happy about that, but it doesn't mean that what's going on here is real. It's not.'

'We're sleeping together.' Abby laughed nervously, ducking to one side and pushing off so that she could swim towards the step, giving herself some time to think and to organise the tumult of thoughts whirring round in her head like angry wasps. She threw over her shoulder, back in control, 'But I understand what you're saying.' She gave him an uneven smile which felt forced. 'Don't worry,' she laughed as her self-control gathered momentum and she forced herself back down to earth, 'I've realised I'm very good when it comes to evading tricky questions without ever resorting to any untruths.'

'I know,' Gabriel said wryly.

'You know?'

'Well, you've managed to spend two years disapproving of my lifestyle without ever saying a word.' He stood up and held out his hand. 'Too much talking. My grandmother won't be up for at least another hour—and, by the way, I approve of the way you managed to entice her into the water. I think she was beginning to nurture fantasies about turning it into a lily pond.' He grinned and instantly forgot the uneasy jarring he had felt earlier on that their conversation had taken an unexpected turn.

'Where are we going?'

'Where do you think?' He pulled her towards him, wet body against wet body, and kissed her with lingering thoroughness. 'I can't get enough of you.'

Same, Abby wanted to tell him, but she didn't. She knew the rules of this game and, whilst he could talk about wanting her, she wasn't sure how happy he would be if she became too expressive on the subject of wanting him back.

He enjoyed her cries of pleasure but there were many lines she knew she couldn't step over, and she wanted to. She wanted to tell him how much she craved him and how much she enjoyed his company—his wit, his intelligence, the feel of his mouth on hers, the expression in his deep, dark eyes when they roved over her body, caressing it in a single look.

She wanted...

She wanted it all.

Heart beating like a steam engine, she followed him into the house, half-trotting along, their fingers linked together.

'You're all about the sex, aren't you?' she said huskily as soon as he had shut the bedroom door and swivelled round to press her back against it, too horny to make it to the bed without touching her first.

'Sex works.' Gabriel pulled down the bikini top and groaned as he cupped her breast in his hand and began playing with it, playing with her nipple, teasing it until it was a stiffened bud and she was breathing fast, sighing those little fluttery sighs that always managed to send his blood pressure through the roof.

And love works even better.

Just thinking that terrified Abby because it was forbidden, against the rules. But, having taken root, it was a pernicious thought that refused to budge and she knew why. As he eased himself down her body, suckling on her nipple, she looked down at his dark head at her breast and despairingly wondered when she had started loving this complex and fascinating man.

Had it all started way back when—before they'd even

come to Seville? Maybe on those dark evenings when they'd ended up working late and, despite having all her defences fully in place, she'd allowed him into her heart? He had the sort of personality that was so persuasive, so captivating. She'd scorned those poor women who'd fallen for him when they'd known full well that he wasn't going to commit to anything more than expensive gifts, chic restaurants and the best seats at the theatre. He was certainly not the sort who would be up for meeting the parents. So why waste time going there? It had seemed very straightforward to Abby! But obviously feelings had a cruel way of ambushing good intentions, and here she was now...

In so deep that it would take a team of scuba divers to pull her out.

She sifted her fingers through his hair and arched back, giving herself to his questing mouth, and panting as he trailed lower down her body until he was buried between her legs, licking, sucking and teasing her with his familiar expertise.

He lifted her off her feet and managed to make it to the bed but his swimming trunks and the linen shirt he had put on by the pool were discarded in record time.

'I can't wait,' he groaned, reaching for protection and applying it with a complete lack of cool.

When he entered her, it was with one forceful thrust, and she groaned in pleasure and clung to him like a limpet as he thrust harder and deeper. Her legs splayed out on either side, bent at the knees, and her whole body was arched back so that her round breasts bounced in time to his love-making.

They'd barely had time to dry off from the pool to

the house and the sound of their semi-wet bodies moving as one was the most erotic sound imaginable.

She had to bury her face against his neck to stop herself from screaming out when she orgasmed because the waves of pleasure rocking her were so intense.

Weak as a kitten, she was aware of him sliding out of her, quickly disposing of the used protection and then returning to the bed to lie next to her.

Wrapped up in the warm, rosy glow of contentment, Abby curled into him and sighed.

She wanted to tell him how much she wished that time would stop for ever, locking them both into this wonderful, satisfying bubble where there was no past and no future, just an everlasting present.

'I should have mentioned this sooner,' Gabriel murmured, 'But I have to be in London tomorrow evening.' He flopped onto his back and stared up at the ceiling.

This wasn't part of the plan but he still wanted her. He wanted *this* when they returned to London. He could have kicked himself for thinking that he could put a time constraint on their relationship but it had seemed a very easy conclusion at the time. He was an expert when it came to detaching and he hadn't foreseen any problem detaching from something that had started life as a charade.

But he hadn't banked on just how addictive she would become. No sooner was he sated than his body was gearing up again to have her, to feel her tightness, abrasive against his girth, and to hear those erotic cries and whimpers that she could never seem to control whenever he touched her.

What would be the ramifications of prolonging this? For the past couple of hours, he had mulled over that scenario and reasoned that it could work. He would be sleeping with his PA, but it wasn't a foregone conclusion that it would jeopardise their working relationship. He had managed to quell his misgivings and look to a bigger picture in which he could continue to sleep with her.

'Tomorrow?' Abby blanched because she had banked on three more days of him.

Gabriel shifted onto his side, prepared to test the water, to ask her how she felt about carrying on once they were back in London. It would certainly delight his grandmother if she came visiting any time soon, which he suspected she would want to do, given her new lease of life.

'I have a meeting that can't be delegated,' he told her ruefully.

'Right. I'd thought…'

'You'd thought…?'

'Well.' She laughed but the laughter stuck in her throat. 'I just thought that we had a bit more time together.'

Gabriel stilled and looked at her narrowly, saying nothing until she shot him a nervous glance from under her lashes.

'Of course,' Abby continued lamely, 'I totally understand about unavoidable meetings. I've worked with you long enough to know where your priorities lie.' Which didn't exactly come out as she'd intended. It had sounded vaguely accusatory, almost as though his priority should have been *her*.

'Where my priorities lie…' Gabriel murmured.

'Your grandmother will be really disappointed.'

'I'll return in a couple of weeks, and then come and

spend weekends here for the foreseeable future. That should appease her.'

'Yes, yes, it will.' Did that include *her*? Abby wondered. She took a deep breath, thought of the safe and careful life she'd led since she'd broken up with Jason. That Internet date had been the most adventurous thing she had done since she had moved to London. She had been so intent on making sure she kept a tight control over her life that she hadn't even noticed just how fast the life she should have been living was passing her by.

Gabriel had awakened her, made her realise how precious each and every moment was, and how important it was that her needs, on all levels, were fulfilled.

So they hadn't talked about London, at least not since they had become lovers. But then, when this had started, they hadn't travelled down roads that had become intimate surprisingly fast, and not just physically intimate, but emotionally intimate.

'Gabriel,' she began huskily, curving her body against his and looking up at him with clear eyes. 'I never thought I could ever feel this way.' She stopped, flushed and thanked the Lord that she hadn't added what had been on the tip of her tongue: *feel this way about you*. She'd stopped in time but she could sense him stilling, reading the unspoken words. 'I mean,' she said helplessly. 'I know what this is about, of course I do, but when I'm here, lying next to you…' Like someone who'd stepped into quicksand, Abby knew that she was floundering, sinking and saying stuff she knew she shouldn't, but somehow she couldn't resist. 'What I'm trying to say… I… I…'

'Don't.'

The single syllable, spoken gently but firmly, was like a boulder dropped into a glassy, flat lake, a boulder that sent ripples cascading in never-ending circles, a cause and effect that brought hot colour flooding her cheeks.

He knew. He'd seen the desperation in her eyes and he was giving her the opportunity to step back from the edge of the cliff.

Abby had never felt so mortified in her life before. She laughed shakily. 'What I was just going to say…' She frantically tried to find a lifeline that wouldn't sound pathetic and contrived. 'Is that, although I find I have feelings for you that I never guessed I could ever have, I've actually…um…missed being at work. It'll be great to get back to reality.'

'Feelings for me?' His voice had cooled. 'No, let's not explore that angle. Let's settle for getting back to the reality waiting for us back in London.' He shifted off the bed and then lazily headed towards the bathroom. 'I'm going to get showered.' He turned to her as he was at the door. 'Then I might have to head to my office downstairs and start ironing out the details for tomorrow's meeting. It's the Jefferson deal. It seems that the family is on board with a takeover but they need to talk it through with me face to face.'

'Yes, the Jefferson deal, right.'

'No rush, but I'll need you to sift through their accounts and forward me the profit margins for the past two years, and which subsidiaries are losing money and how much.'

'Yes, of course.' She clutched the sheet to her and wriggled into a sitting position. Her bland, efficient face was back in place but in fact he wasn't even looking at

her. He'd disappeared into the bathroom and she heard
the decisive click of the door being locked.

Their time was at an end. He'd caught a whiff of
something he hadn't wanted, a whiff of her wanting
what they had to continue, to see where it might lead,
and he had scarpered faster than a speeding bullet. To
his credit, he had stopped her from making an absolute fool of herself from which there would have been
no going back.

On tenterhooks, Abby got dressed and eventually
headed downstairs, to find him in the kitchen, chatting to his grandmother. He'd broken the news of their
premature departure but had obviously buttered her up
with promises to return.

His dark eyes on her were remote and polite. When
he dutifully put his arms around her, in a show of intimacy Ava had come to expect, Abby could feel his distance as powerfully as a punch in the stomach.

And, just in case she hadn't got the message, he
didn't accompany her upstairs when it was time for bed.

'My report is going to take a while,' he said as they
stared at one another, she about to head upstairs and he
about to move off into the opposite direction.

'Is it?' Abby asked quietly.

'Yes, Abby. It is. You would do well not to wait up
for me.' He'd come that close to inviting her into his
life for a bit longer. He would have done it. He would
have risked his professional relationship with her because he still wanted her. Gabriel couldn't believe that
he had allowed himself to drop his guard the way he
had purely because the sex had been so good. Was it
because the circumstances were so extraordinary? Was

that why he had behaved out of character? There could
be no other explanation for it.

Now she was looking at him with calm, grey eyes,
and he knew that if he looked hard enough he would
see the hurt there. He raked his fingers through his hair
and glanced away.

Abby felt caught between wanting to bring this all
out into the open, lance the boil so to speak, and needing to close the lid on it before things were said and
emotions declared that could never be taken back.

Close the lid, she thought, and at least she could continue with her job. Where else would she find another
like it? It would be hard seeing him every day, and picking things up where they'd been left off when so much
had changed between them, but she could do it. In a
way, it might even be beneficial to see him return to his
bad old ways, wining and dining his voluptuous dates
before growing tired of them and dispatching them to
Never-Never Land.

She would be able to put everything into perspective and move on, having endured the most important
learning curve of her life.

And if he found someone he wanted to make a permanent fixture in his life?

Abby felt her stomach lurch, as though she'd hit the
top of the rollercoaster ride and was now swooping
down with the ground flying towards her.

'Sure,' she said stiffly, hovering. He looked so damn
awkward. She could practically feel the pity wafting off
him in waves, and she tightened her mouth and straightened her back. 'I forgot to mention,' she said politely,
'That I spoke to my dad about the money. I had some
doubts that he would take it, but I managed to convince

him that it was a windfall win on a lottery ticket and that I would be upset if he didn't use it to make life comfortable for them once they get back from their round-the-world cruise.'

'Lottery ticket?' Gabriel was amused in spite of himself. 'He fell for that?'

'People believe what they want to believe,' she said wryly, quoting him back at himself, and he shook his head because for just a moment there was a perfect understanding between them that made him want to walk towards her and kiss away every single thing that had been said since he'd left the bed and declared that work was beckoning.

'Right.' He pushed off and began heading towards the other wing of the villa.

'Right,' Abby parroted, turning away. 'I'll make sure I'm packed and ready to leave first thing.'

The bedroom had never felt so lonely, not even on that first night when she had stared with horror at a bed she was consigned to share with him. She had curled up on her side, trying to create as much distance between them, and had contemplated the time ahead with dread.

Now, bath done, hair washed and bags packed, she crept between the sheets and felt the emptiness next to her with something approaching despair.

She had no one to blame but herself, not that that was any consolation.

She had no idea when he came to bed but, despite tossing and turning and thinking that there was no way she could ever fall asleep—not when her nerves were all over the place—she must have nodded off because when she woke the following morning there was an indentation where he had lain, although he was nowhere to be seen.

Downstairs, she thought, ensconced in his office, catching up on all those important deals that suddenly needed sorting out. Anything to spare himself the embarrassment of having to face her because he'd seen that she had wanted to carry on a fling that had reached the end of its lifespan.

His case was by the front door, and she was looking at it when he emerged from the direction of the office at the far end of the villa.

'I should go and get my bag,' Abby said, half-turning.

'No rush. I'll bring it down when we're ready to go.'

'I… I wasn't sure what to do with the clothes you bought for me here,' she told him. 'So I've left them in the wardrobe.'

'Why?' Gabriel looked at her, arms folded. 'What am I supposed to do with a collection of women's designer clothes?'

'Don't know,' Abby told him with cool self-control. 'I don't honestly care, Gabriel. I wore them here to play a part but they're not my style.'

'Well, my grandmother will be startled if she opens the cupboard and finds that you've left half the stuff you've been wearing behind.' He thought of that little bikini coming off, the pale green dress he had lifted so that he could get to her knickers, his whole body on full throttle, so hot for her that he'd scarcely been able to control himself. He clenched his jaw and looked away.

'Well, it might provide a good opportunity for you to break the sad news of our break-up.' She glanced at her finger where the engagement ring still glittered and gleamed. She would remove it just as soon as they were on their way back to reality. Right now, though, the twinkling diamonds were a mocking reminder of her foolishness.

Gabriel shrugged. 'Fine. I'll dispose of them.' He paused, then stared at her with narrowed eyes. 'I hope this episode isn't going to alter our working relationship, Abby. Things happened, but I'm sincerely hoping that you'll be able to put it all behind you.'

Abby noted that, by inference, he had already put it all behind *him*. She also wondered whether there'd been a threat implied by that bland remark. Was he implying that he would have to let her go otherwise?

Pride slammed into her and she returned his stare with one that was equally controlled. 'Absolutely,' she said. 'Whatever mistaken impression you may have got, the whole episode, as you call it, is already behind me.'

CHAPTER NINE

Book me a table at my usual restaurant, Abby.
Two people.
Corner seat.

ABBY STARED DOWN at Gabriel's distinctive writing. He'd left a note while she'd been out to lunch and she knew that he wouldn't be back in until the following morning—meetings all afternoon.

Indeed, she had barely laid eyes on him since they'd returned from Seville ten days previously. True to his word, he had returned to spend the weekend with his grandmother. She had arranged his private jet. What had transpired? Had he told Ava that their engagement was no more? Abby didn't know, because he hadn't said a word about it, and that had made her unreasonably angry because damn it, she'd *liked* his grandmother, had *bonded* with her.

It was as though the minute she'd left Spain she'd left behind everything relating to it, so updates on how Ava was doing were no longer relevant.

They'd boarded the plane to London, she'd handed him back the engagement ring and that had been that.

Back to normal. Back to routine. Back to work.

He was once more her boss, except now there were subtle changes in their relationship. Of course he still relied on her to get everything right, and to do whatever overtime was needed. And he still trusted her enough barely to check the work she did. But gone was the lazy banter and that easy familiarity which she was only recognising, now that it was gone, had been there for ever.

He was polite but she knew that they were circling one another like strangers and it was killing her.

Was it likewise killing him?

No chance. She looked at the scribbled note and knew exactly what it meant. He was back in the dating game. That restaurant was his restaurant of choice when it came to dining out with a woman and the corner table was his preferred spot.

Abby took a few deep breaths and closed her eyes. She would book the table but this was the end of the road for her. She'd thought she could do this, could carry on working for him, putting things into perspective. She'd thought that the minute he started seeing other women it would be a resounding reminder of the sort of guy he was, deep down. Yes, he was a thousand things, a complex mosaic of personality traits that would turn any woman's head, but primarily he was a commitment-phobe and a commitment-phobe was the last thing she needed.

Where a soul should be, was a block of ice. In the end, she'd counted for nothing.

She picked up the phone and dialled the special number she used that would ensure a corner table just as he liked it...

Gabriel stood at his office window, looking down but not really seeing the ebb and flow of people filling the pavements below. The expensive dinner he had booked the night before had been a resounding flop. His date had been too much of everything he hadn't wanted: too tall, too busty, too flamboyant, too downright stupid, too self-obsessed. He'd been bored stiff after fifteen minutes and had only sat through the terminally dull evening through a sense of common courtesy.

She had been visibly gutted when he had sent her on her merry way at a little after eleven.

Maybe, he thought, it was time for him to move on from flamboyant, fun creatures, because it was patently obvious that the fun element of them had vanished.

He scowled and looked at his watch, then was annoyed with himself for doing that, because he knew that at the back of his mind he was checking to see how long it might be before Abby arrived.

He'd thought that a spot of replacement therapy might help put memories of her to rest. They were back in London, he'd reasoned. Even though his grandmother had yet to be told that the engagement was off, he'd felt the need to move on, to take back up the reins of his love life, which would include riffling through his little black book and going on a date.

The very second Abby had told him that she had feelings for him, he'd known that he had to step away. She'd tried to back away from a confession that had been spoken without editing, but it had been too late to take back what had been thoughtlessly blurted out.

There was not going to be a full-fledged relationship leading anywhere. He wasn't up for that and he never would be. He'd made that clear. She might deny that that was what she wanted, but he'd known.

What choice had he had but to extricate himself?

He was never going to become a hopeless loser who handed over his emotional freedom to someone else. He was never going to allow anyone to have the power to hurt him. He had nurtured his independence and he wasn't about to jettison it for anyone. He just wasn't built that way, and he certainly wasn't going to launch into any touchy-feely explanations as to why not.

She'd got herself into a mess, and that was unfortunate, but there you go. Life was full of unfortunate events.

But he hadn't banked on bloody missing her just the way he did. He hadn't banked on how tough it would be seeing her around the office, back to her usual cool, detached, smiling self. He'd perversely wished that she'd display at least *some* misery that their fling was over. He wondered whether he hadn't overreacted, misread the signals. She was as cool as a cucumber around the office! Maybe he'd been wrong.

But Gabriel had unshakeable faith in his own powers of detection and knew that he'd done the right thing. He was just frustrated that he couldn't put her behind him as easily as he had previous women and he surmised that that was because what they had had come to a premature end.

He still wanted her. It was no wonder she was still in his head! He was accustomed to ending relationships and then breathing a sigh of relief. He wasn't accustomed to ending something that still had legs.

Yes, he knew it was egotistic thinking along those lines, but he couldn't help it.

Which was why he was here now, gazing sightlessly down at the crowds below and thinking about a woman who had no place in his life.

'Busy, Gabriel? I can come back later, but I'd like to have a word with you.'

Gabriel spun round. 'You're early.' He glanced at his watch, then looked at her. The shimmering bright colours and skimpy clothes she had worn in Seville had been replaced by the usual drab office gear: grey skirt, neat grey jacket, black pumps and an off-white blouse with little pearly buttons down the front.

He pushed himself away from the window and headed to his desk to sit. 'Problems with those reports I emailed you?'

'I've done all of that, Gabriel. No problems there.' Abby shoved an envelope towards him but, instead of sitting down, she remained where she was.

'What's that?'

'You should open it.'

'Why?'

'Why what?' She laughed nervously, her eyes skittering away from his. 'Why should you open it? Why am I here? Why is the world round?' Nerves were making her jabber. She knew that, and she knew that it wasn't just nerves. It was a combination of nerves and abject misery at the next chapter of her life she was facing.

'Why do you feel the need to resign?'

'How do you know…?'

Gabriel linked his fingers together and relaxed back into his chair. 'What else is it going to be, Abby?' He reached forward, picked up the envelope, slit it open and read the contents aloud. 'Grateful for the opportunities…desire to look in other directions…have thoroughly enjoyed time here…blah, blah, blah…

'So?' he pressed, not moving a muscle, his dark eyes pinning her to the spot. In a gesture that was totally uncool, Gabriel crumpled the letter of resignation and tossed it across his desk. Abby lurched forward and grabbed it before it could hit the floor.

She sat down in her usual chair facing his desk, meticulously uncrumpled the brief letter of resignation and busied herself smoothing it out.

'I...'

'Have decided that there are better jobs out there? More exciting career prospects? More...thrilling opportunities?' he completed harshly.

Abby's grey eyes were calm as she looked up at him and met his fulminating gaze.

So, he was angry. She'd more or less expected that because she knew, without any vanity, that he valued their working relationship and would find it annoying to go through the hassle of finding someone else, especially given his none-too-fabulous track record when it came to hiring PAs.

Tough.

'There are always alternative opportunities out there when it comes to work, Gabriel, and of course I'll make sure that I find a suitable replacement.'

'Jesus, Abby, is that *all* you have to say?' He slammed his fist on the table and pushed back his chair to stand up. He looked at her for a few seconds then began pacing the huge office, scowling, while Abby twisted round to look at him.

She'd taken ages to compose the eight-line letter of resignation, longer, indeed, than it had taken her to decide to resign in the first place.

Booking that intimate table at that intimate restaurant had sealed the deal for her. She'd thought she could see things through and philosophise her way past her heartache, but she'd been wrong, and there was no point clinging to the hope that that might change any time soon. She was in love with a man who didn't return her love and it was never going to get better unless she left.

'What else do you want me to say, Gabriel?'

'I can tell you what I *don't* want you to say!' He planted himself directly in her line of vision and glared.

'What's that?'

'What I *don't* want is a load of crap about *more exciting opportunities* and *thanks for the good times…*'

Abby stared down at the creased piece of paper on her lap. Her eyes blurred. What did he want from her? The truth? Anger coursed through her and she raised her eyes to him, met his thunderous glare with cold disapproval.

'Does it matter what words I use, Gabriel? I can't work for you any more. That's the long and short of it.'

Resuming his restless pacing of the office before coming to perch on the edge of the desk, and then, as though that might be too relaxed a position for him, swerving once again to sit in his leather swivel chair, Gabriel shot back, 'You told me that you would be able to resume working with me without any problems.'

'I was wrong. Okay?'

'As far as I can see, we've been doing just fine.'

'Please don't make this more difficult than it needs to be, Gabriel. I'll make sure my replacement is as good as I am. I'll fill her, *or him*, in on every single account and how to manage them.'

'Why couldn't you just stick to the programme?' Gabriel looked at her with frustration, almost as surprised as she was to hear himself utter that question.

'Because I'm not you,' Abby replied in a low voice.

'And, yes, I really thought that I could keep my emotions out of it, but in the end I couldn't.' She looked him squarely in the face. So he wanted an explanation? Then she would give him one, but not until she was sure that the minute she walked out of that office she would not be walking back into it, replacement or no replacement.

'Gabriel,' she hesitated, 'I don't suppose you know this, but I'm due holiday.'

'Come again?'

'I've stored up quite a bit of holiday which I haven't got around to taking. Five weeks, in fact.'

'You haven't been on holiday for the past year?'

'I've had weekends here and there but, no, I haven't had a stretch of time off for quite a while. With my mother not being well, I've found it better to go down to see them as often as I can.'

'What does that have to do with anything?'

'What I'm saying is, because I've just had snatched weekends here and there, I have holiday to take and I'm going to take it so that I can leave sooner. I'm sorry if you think this is the equivalent of leaving you in the lurch, because I won't be devoting time to finding my replacement, but I don't think it's going to work, my staying on here any longer than I have to.'

She drew in a deep, steadying breath. 'Under normal circumstances, I would have stayed until I found someone suitable to replace me, but these aren't normal circumstances unfortunately. I know you're probably put out but I'm hoping that you do the decent thing and release me without trying to find ways of making me stay. I don't mean to blow hot and cold but…things have been said that can't be unsaid. My position here is now untenable.'

She thought of walking through that office door, never to walk back through it again. Never to see him again. Never to smile at something witty he might have said, never to appreciate that wry sense of humour or to shoot him one of her disapproving looks when he teased her just a little too close to the bone. Not that there had been any of that since they'd returned from Seville.

'I can't think of anything worse than chaining you to your desk and making you work out your notice when you'd rather walk away without turning back.'

'I won't feel guilty about this, Gabriel.'

'I knew it was a mistake for us to...' He shook his head. When he looked down at his hand, he frowned because it was unsteady.

Understandable. Where the hell was he going to find someone as good as she was? This was exactly what came of allowing your head to take a vacation and let your baser instincts an opportunity to come out and play.

'Is that what you think?'

'What are you talking about?'

'Is that what you think—that what we did was a mistake?'

'Not the game we played for the sake of my grand-mother.' Gabriel loathed this sort of emotional conversa-tio. He was a man of action, someone solution-oriented. Frankly what was the point of talking about something when there was no solution to put on the table? There was no solution here, but the way she was gazing at him, her eyes calm and steady...

'She...needed what we did,' he continued roughly.

'And have you got round to telling her that we're no longer going out—involved? Engaged?'

Gabriel flushed darkly. 'It's not been a fortnight,' he muttered. 'If I return to London only to phone her up and break the bad news, then she's going to start imagining that it might have been something she said, or did.'

'So how long do you give it?'

'Does it matter, Abby?' he asked with mounting irritation. 'It's hardly as though you're going to be around to deal with any fallout.'

'No,' Abby breathed in deeply. 'You're right. It doesn't matter because I won't be around to deal with the fallout.' But that didn't mean that she didn't feel awful about it, because she did. 'But I wasn't asking that. I wasn't asking whether you regretted the little pretend game we played for Ava's sake. I was asking whether you regretted what happened next.'

Gabriel could sense when he was being led into a trap and this felt like that. What did she want him to say? 'There's very little in life I regret,' he drawled, in absolute command of the conversation and refusing to be manoeuvred into any dodgy side alleys. 'Things happen.' He shrugged and looked at her until she was the first to break eye contact. 'We made love. We're adults. Retrospectively, had I known that you would find yourself unable to deal with the consequences...' He let the remainder of that observation hang in the air between them.

'That's regret by any other name,' Abby said, drawing in a deep breath. 'Well, if I'd had a crystal ball at the time, then who knows? Maybe I would have steered clear of any involvement. But maybe, Gabriel, I would have done the same thing. Because, believe it or not, I don't regret what we did, not for a minute.'

Their eyes tangled and Gabriel felt a tug of admiration for her honesty. Many others would have taken the easy route out of this situation. Good job…fat pay cheque…go with the flow. Some, he thought cynically, might have gone down a different road. He'd slept with an employee. Some might have thought a little blackmail to be in order…or a lucrative kiss-and-tell story to a seedy tabloid… Wouldn't have worked, of course, but money could be a powerful motivator when it came to underhand behaviour.

Abby wasn't going to go with the flow and he wasn't very surprised because everything about her, as he had discovered, spoke of someone who didn't shy away from facing consequences. She'd had her heart broken but she hadn't hidden under a rock to lick her wounds. She had picked herself up and left everything she had ever known to make her way in a city she had probably visited once or twice in her life. She hadn't become a pathetic wreck and she hadn't thought of forgetting her ex by flinging herself straight into the arms of anyone who might help take her mind off her hurt. No, she had developed a steely front to protect herself and gone from there.

And now…

'I don't blame you,' she said quietly. 'You were upfront. You told me like it was and I ended up barging past all the "don't trespass" signs because I was falling in love with you.' She could feel the heat scorching her cheeks but, when she walked out that door, she wanted to walk out with no misunderstandings between them. She wanted the air to be completely clear.

'Falling in love…feelings you had for me… You said…' Gabriel raked his fingers through his hair.

'Yes, and I could see on your face that when I let

that slip it was most certainly not what you wanted to hear, but there you go. I'm in love with you and that's why I can't carry on working for you. I made that booking for the restaurant and that was the end of the road for me.'

'You always maintained that I wasn't your type.'

'You're not,' Abby said shortly. 'Which just goes to show that there's no such thing as common sense when it comes to matters of the heart. You can do your check list and still end up getting ambushed by someone who just doesn't tick all the boxes.'

'That's not a mistake I will ever make.' Gabriel wondered whether that remark had been deliberately pointed but he didn't think so, not judging from the way she was looking at him, clear-eyed and direct. No clinging, no neediness, no pleading for chances that weren't on the cards.

'I'll stay the day, Gabriel. Tidy things, make a list that my replacement might find handy. And I can talk to Rita in Human Resources. I'll tell her the sort of person who might fit the bill. She's brilliant.'

Gabriel raked his fingers through his hair. 'And what if I tell you that I'm going to demand you work your notice?'

'Are you?'

'Of course I'm not.' He shook his head and stood up. 'And you needn't worry that I might be tempted to give you anything but a glowing reference.'

'I know,' Abby said. 'You're nothing if not fair.' She got to her feet as well to stand behind her chair, gripping the back and looking at him, *drinking him in for one last time*.

'I would ask you to reconsider,' Gabriel told her,

'But, given everything you've said, it's probably for the best that you go.'

Can't have your PA drooling over you, Abby thought acidly. *We both know where that leads—straight to the unemployment office.*

She'd been honest, but she was going to leave with her head held high and her pride intact. She hadn't committed a crime by falling in love with him, not unless you could call being a complete idiot a crime.

'I hope you let your grandmother know how fond I was of her, Gabriel. And, just in case you're tempted to feel sorry for me, I've thought this through and I'm looking forward to what lies ahead.'

'Who said anything about feeling sorry for you?' Gabriel flushed darkly and wondered what shiny future she was looking forward to. He certainly wasn't interested in hearing about any shiny future that involved men. 'I'm sure you'll land a pretty spectacular job without too much trouble.'

'Job?' Abby blinked.

'You said that you were looking forward to what lies ahead…'

'Oh, yes. Sure. Yes, I think there are some exciting opportunities out there, and it's going to stand me in very good stead that I've worked with you and for your company.'

She hadn't been talking about a new job or exciting opportunities, Gabriel thought sourly. She'd been talking about a different type of excitement lying in store for her, the sort of excitement he wasn't interested in hearing about.

He walked towards the door that connected their two

offices, his the much larger. Then he paused, his hand on the door knob.

'I'm not good for any woman who wants the fairy-tale ending. You're better off without a man like me,' Gabriel said roughly. She was looking up at him, her eyes wide and clear, her skin still golden from the days spent out in Seville. He wanted to reach out and yank her towards him, which just went to show how irrational the whole business of lust could be.

'I think I probably am,' Abby replied truthfully. 'But I'm grateful to you, Gabriel.'

'How so?'

'I'd locked myself away after my broken engagement, gone into protective mode. When I finally told myself that I had to get back out there into the dating pool again, I had so many clauses and conditions for the kind of guy I was looking for that there was no room left for spontaneity. You showed me that there's no such thing as the perfect guy.'

'Is there a compliment buried in there somewhere?'

'I'll get over you,' Abby said with a lot more confidence than she was feeling. 'Because we all get over broken hearts, and the next time I get involved with someone I won't make a tally of the things they have or don't have. I shall just go with the flow and accept that relationships don't have to lead to anything. You made me appreciate the concept of just having fun. Yes, I fell for you, but what I'll take away is the fact that I learned how to be impulsive—I think for the first time in my life.'

'Good.'

'And you're moving on too,' Abby couldn't resist adding, wanting and needing to feel the twist of the knife inside her when he admitted that he'd found her replacement. 'But then I don't think you're the kind of guy to ever let the grass grow under his feet.'

Gabriel scowled darkly when he thought about his disaster date. 'I'm going to head out,' he said, strolling to fetch his jacket which had been tossed on one of the chairs. 'You can leave whenever you like, but make sure there's someone here to cover the essentials.' He began slipping on the jacket as he walked back towards her. 'I'd say,' he murmured, 'Thanks for the good times, but I think that might sound a little too B-movie.' He reached out. He couldn't help himself. The urge to feel the smooth, satiny curve of her cheek was irresistible.

He felt her stillness under his hand. Her eyelids fluttered and she took a wobbly step back, but it was as if his magnetic pull was too powerful for her, because she remained staring up at him, her lips parted, her grey eyes wide and panicked.

Her whole body thrummed with forbidden sexual awareness.

He was going to kiss her.

Abby felt his intent and saw it in the darkening of his eyes. He let his gaze drop to do a leisurely tour of her face and her body, then back to her face, and still her stupid legs seemed to have forgotten the basic principles of movement.

Did he think that he could make a pass at her after she'd poured her heart out? She'd told him she was in love with him, and he'd informed her that that just wasn't going to do and, yes, it was the right thing for her to clear off.

So *how dared he* now touch her like this and set her

whole body ablaze with a craven yearning that could never, ever reach a satisfactory conclusion?

Did he imagine that he could take what he wanted because she was vulnerable? Because she was in love with him?

She jerked back and turned away, but she was shaking like a leaf, and had to take a few deep, steadying breaths to get herself back under control.

'I don't think so,' she told him coldly. 'You don't get to touch me.' She jerked open the door and scooted through, heading straight for the safety of her desk, behind which she remained standing to look at him, cool and remote. Inside, however, she was a mess.

She tilted her chin up and maintained eye contact. 'I'll make sure that Rita is on the case first thing in the morning to find a replacement.'

Caught having to subdue a runaway libido, Gabriel nodded curtly and walked towards the door. 'Good luck with your job search, Abby, and whatever other searches you intend to indulge.' He looked at her, her flushed face, the rigid stance of her body, the proud angle of her head, and he was assailed by a tidal wave of memories that were both uninvited and unwanted. 'Oh, and leave your company laptop and phone with HR, would you? Company policy.'

And with that he was gone, quietly shutting the door behind him, exiting her life without a sound.

Abby remained staring at the closed door for several minutes. She marvelled that the life that had absorbed every ounce of her being for close to two years could disappear as quickly as it had. Gabriel's personality was so huge that he seemed to leave a physical void behind him.

He wasn't going to reappear. He'd be gone for the remainder of the day, and he was going to remain gone so that, by the time he next stepped foot into his office, there would be no risk of seeing her still there.

Even so, Abby worked fast to complete everything she felt should be done in record time.

She'd made a couple of acquaintances at the office and, in due course, she would get in touch and paper over her hurried resignation with some fabricated story, but for now only Rita would know that she was leaving, and Rita was as silent as the grave.

'You'll have to find someone as quickly as possible to replace me,' Abby told her. 'Someone…who…well…'

'Someone who can cope with him.' Rita smiled, understanding completely, but not pressing her for an explanation.

That hurt, because it reminded Abby of how well she and Gabriel had worked together, and in the end how well they had played together. She had to fight down the temptation to burst into tears.

'He can be difficult,' she said, 'But he's never unkind and he's always fair. You'll just need to get someone with…stamina.' Which was something she'd thought she had until he'd got under her skin and burrowed into her heart.

She was mentally washed out by the time she returned to her house and the enthusiasm to do anything at all had gone. She couldn't be bothered to search for jobs on the Internet. She could scarcely be bothered to fix herself something to eat.

She wanted to curl up into a ball and disappear for a few hours. Or days or weeks…

Should she have let him kiss her? One last touch

before the big goodbye? She dwelled on what it would have been like to feel his lips on hers one last time. She went to sleep wondering where she could find the inner strength to deal with the fact that she would never see him again.

Find it she would, because she had no choice, but after a week of distracted job-hunting and far too many lie-ins Abby admitted defeat and decided that she would take herself down to her parents'. They were on their cruise. She would have the house to herself and maybe, away from the hustle and bustle of London, she would be able to get her act together. There was no great rush to get a job, as she had ample savings which she had been putting aside for a deposit on a place or a rainy day. This certainly qualified as a rainy day, as far as she was concerned.

And maybe she wouldn't bother returning to London. There was no need to, was there? She could look for something locally, or maybe further afield in Exeter. She would be able to afford to buy a lot more down there than in the capital.

She would be miles away from Gabriel with no possibility of ever running into him by chance.

And her broken heart would be given the space to heal.

CHAPTER TEN

ABBY STARTED TO the sound of the doorbell just as she had slipped into her pyjamas. It was going to be another early night but that was what deep, dark country living did to someone trying to piece together a broken heart. Outside, there were no street lights to illuminate the twisting road off which her parents' house sat, squat, square and reassuringly familiar.

After ten days out here, she had finally got up the courage to tell her parents that she had quit her job and was now back in Somerset. She'd had no choice because sooner or later someone from the small village would have emailed them. Returning to her tiny home town was great when it came to wrapping herself up in the comfort blanket of what she knew, but terrible when it came to hiding out.

For a few seconds, she debated whether she should get the door or else just pretend that she wasn't in, except that was something else that was impossible to achieve in a small home-town—invisibility. If she wasn't in the house, then *where was she*?

Not to answer the door would have been to risk a search party being dispatched to try and seek her out.

So off she went, detouring to sling her dressing gown

over the drab pyjamas, because she hadn't been able to bring herself to put on anything sexier.

There was no peep hole through which she could identify an uninvited guest.

She opened the door a fraction, because London had taught her to be careful when it came to doorbells pinging at nine-thirty in the evening.

Leather shoes, patent and expensive. Trousers, grey and *unspeakably* expensive. A hand shoved into one of the trouser pockets, distorting it. Abby's eyes lingered on that hand, the way the dark hair curled round the dull matt of a steel watch.

Everything in her head was adding up to the identity of her caller, yet she refused to believe what her eyes were telling, her because the last person she expected to see standing on the doorstep of her parents' house was Gabriel.

Gabriel could read what was going through her head. Like everything else, every other detail quietly stored away over time, this was just another one of those little things that should have pointed to the direction in which his emotions were going. He knew her. He knew her without even realising that he knew her—just as she knew him—and that was something he'd found out in the eerie quiet of his office, with his efficient replacement PA whose presence only served to remind him of the woman who was no longer there. He'd caught himself missing Abby's smile, the way she could read what he was going to say, the way *she was*. He'd been so sure of himself, so naively convinced that he was invulnerable when it came to falling in love, so *bloody stupid*.

She was still half-hiding behind the door. With utter shock and the dizzying sensation that soon the ground was going to give way under her feet, Abby finally raised disbelieving eyes to his face and her heart stood still. He had been on her mind every second of every minute of every day, yet how was it that she had failed to remember just how stunningly beautiful he was? How tall? How sinfully sexy? He was smiling that crooked little smile that made her toes curl and her tummy lurch.

How dared he land on her doorstep with that smile?

Abby stiffened and moved slightly to bar him further from entering the house.

'You,' she said coldly. 'What are you doing here?'

Gabriel looked at her without budging. Good question, he thought, except there was no single-syllable answer to it.

Deserted by the easy charm and abundant self-assurance that was so much part and parcel of his personality, he could only stare at her.

This was pretty much what he'd imagined her night wear to look like—before the sexy lingerie had come out into the open. Baggy pyjamas, strange, fluffy bedroom slippers, faded dressing gown...

Except she looked even sexier in this get up than she had in any of the skimpy silk-and-lace froth she had worn when they'd been in Seville.

He clenched his jaw and diverted his eyes from the jut of her breasts under the layers of clothes.

'I've come to...talk to you.'

'Really? What about?'

'Will you let me in?' He tried to peer around her. 'I'm guessing your parents haven't returned from their cruise?'

'How did you find out where I was?'

'You neighbour. She was very helpful when she found out that I was your boss and that I needed to see you.'

'Sophie should never, *never*, have revealed my whereabouts!'

'Maybe she didn't see me as a threatening predator up to no good.'

Abby glowered at him. She refused to get stuck in a stupid conversation about what her neighbour in London might or might not have thought of Gabriel. He was drop-dead gorgeous and would have swanned up in one of his mega-expensive cars. Add to that the fact that he could ooze charm at the snap of a finger, and it was little wonder that Sophie had cracked and told him where she was.

'You haven't told me what you're doing here.'

'Abby...' Firmly on the back foot, Gabriel sifted his fingers through his hair and shook his head. 'This isn't a conversation I want to have standing on your doorstep. Let me come in. Please.'

It was the *please* that did it. That and the fact that Gabriel on her doorstep would set the gossip grapevine on fire should anyone happen to pass by and spot him.

'If this is to do with work,' Abby said as soon as he was in the hallway, 'Then I can't help you. I left Rita with as many instructions as I could and it's up to her to sort you out with someone suitable.' She wasn't looking at him. She didn't dare. She didn't even want to be in his radius so she shuffled a little towards the wall and folded her arms.

She didn't know why Gabriel had come, and she didn't want to start thinking that it had anything to do with wanting to see *her*, which just left work, and that made perfect sense because it was about the only thing he was capable of caring about.

'It's not to do with work. Look, I've just spent hours on the road. Could we sit…somewhere?'

'I don't recall inviting you here, Gabriel, so why would I invite you to make yourself at home?' She stared at him narrowly and then, with an impatient sigh, she walked towards the kitchen because *she* needed to sit down, never mind him.

Gabriel followed. Hostility sparked from every bone in her body and he couldn't blame her.

'You can have a cup of coffee,' Abby said, struggling to keep herself together, even though her mind was whizzing through every possible reason that might have brought him down here. 'And then you can go.' She banged around for a couple of minutes, made two mugs of coffee and turned to find him seated at the kitchen table.

Uncomfortable as he appeared to be, he still owned the space around him, and that made her even angrier because this was *her* territory, *her* refuge and he couldn't just come here and somehow *take over*.

She'd told him how she felt about him and then she had walked away. *With his blessing!* The cogs in her brain turned and bits began falling into place. If he wasn't here because he needed to find a file, then he could only be here for one other reason.

Abby reddened as her anger levels shot through the roof.

'I know why you're here,' she said in a low, trembling voice. She sat down, facing him, hands cupping the mug. 'When I last saw you, Gabriel, you were moving on, getting back on the horse! So? Did your hot date not live up to expectation?' Abby taunted, wallowing in the pain because it fuelled her anger and that in turn protected her from the sickening impact he had on her, despite everything.

'She did not.'

'Oh, dear! What a shame! Well, Gabriel, if you think that you can swan down here and pick up where we left off because you've found that my replacement hasn't worked out the way you thought it would, then you're mistaken. *I don't want anything else to do with you. Ever.*'

'I'm not here to pick up where we left off,' Gabriel said quietly. 'And I certainly wouldn't think of presuming to tempt you back into a relationship because I've decided that I still want you.'

'Good!' Except what on earth was he doing here in that case? 'Is...is Ava all right?' she asked uncertainly.

'We're going round the houses, Abby. I came here to...talk to you. I wish I knew where to begin but this is difficult for me.'

'Gabriel, are *you* all right?' Fear clutched her and she had to stop herself from leaping out of her chair and flinging herself at him.

He smiled crookedly. 'Health wise, I'm in top condition. As I once remember telling you, there's not a germ that could get past my defences. I would never allow it.'

Bewildered, Abby stared at him. Shorn of his natural panache, there was a vulnerability about him that made the breath catch in her throat, and she didn't want that. She didn't want him getting to her in any way. She'd fought tooth and nail to try and move forward, and had spent so many hours polishing the check list of all the reasons why she was better off without him that the thought of that check list being dismantled filled her with despair.

She just didn't want him sitting there, looking beautiful and somehow *uncertain*, and making her play guessing games.

'Well, I don't know why you're here, but *don't* you try and use clever words to get round me.'

'For once, I find that I've run out of clever words,' Gabriel said with such seriousness that Abby blinked in confusion, fighting down the crazy hope that had sprang from nowhere and was making itself heard. Her heart was beating like a sledgehammer. She licked her lips, eyes fixed on him. 'You told me how you felt, Abby, and I did what I was programmed to do—I ran in the opposite direction. I wasn't interested in any sort of emotional involvement and I wasn't about to open that up for discussion. That's how it had always been and nothing was going to change on that front.'

He sighed. 'I've spent my life standing back from making the mistake of letting go. In truth, it had never been very difficult, because I'd never met anyone I was remotely interested in letting go *to*, if you get my meaning. Until you.'

'Don't, Gabriel. Please don't say things you don't mean.'

'It's the truth. I knew that one day I would marry, because I knew it was what my grandmother wanted—it was expected, but I was arrogant enough to assume that I could have that without going down the road of emotional commitment. All other types of commitment, yes, but not the kind that could lead me to become weak and vulnerable, the way my father had become weak and vulnerable when it came to my mother. Not that kind. My father's love for my mother seemed to count above all else—above his love for his son, even. And, when he lost her, the *grief* took over everything for him, too. I planned to never succumb to that kind of love.'

He laughed shortly. 'Then I became involved with you. The one person who had shared my life more than any woman had ever done. You brought me news of my fiancée and, instead of being distraught, I was quietly relieved. Lucy, on paper, would have made the perfect wife but she wanted more than I would ever have been prepared to give. I was immune to emotional involvement. I'd locked my heart away and thrown out the key, which is why, when we became lovers, it never occurred to me that there would be anything more to it for me than sex. Brilliant sex, as it turned out. Brilliant, once in a lifetime, unbeatable, fireworks-in-the-sky sex.'

Abby thought about that fireworks-in-the-sky sex and her whole body tingled as though he'd reached out and stroked her.

She didn't know where this was going and she was too addled to try and predict the destination. Too addled and too wrapped up looking at him, hating him for coming, and loving him for it at the same time.

'I never thought that, against all odds, the very thing I'd spent a lifetime avoiding would creep up from behind and take me by surprise,' he said roughly. 'I ended up wanting so much more when I was with you. What started as a game became...what can I say? It turned into reality. I did just what I'd warned you not to do.'

'What do you mean?'

'Alarm bells should have sounded,' Gabriel said wryly, 'When I realised that whatever it was driving me to take you was way beyond my control.'

'It was?'

'That time in Seville was a revelation, even though I chose to bury that realisation and put it down to great sex and nothing more. My grandmother tells me that she knew you were the one the minute she met you and saw the way we interacted. Unfortunately, I only knew you were the one for me when I realised that I'd lost you. That date? Fiasco. The only woman I wanted to be with was you, and you were the woman I had turned my back on because I was too stupid to and stubborn to face the fact that what you felt for me was what I felt for you.'

'You love me?'

'I have no words to describe how much, Abby. My life has been a mess since you left.'

'So, you love me…and you're not just saying that?'

'So I do, and I'm not.' He gave her a lopsided grin that went straight to her heart. Now the distance separating them felt like a canyon and all she wanted to do was bridge the gap and get close to him, touch him. 'You have no idea what it felt like driving down here,' he said gravely. 'I'd messed up big time and I'm prepared to beg you to give me a second chance, let me prove to you that I'm worth it.'

'Now I'm going to cry.'

'That's what I have a shoulder for. For you to cry on.' He patted his lap and she shuffled over to sit on it and throw her arms round his neck, content to nestle into him. 'I came here to ask you to marry me. A real engagement, a real wedding and all the fuzzy stuff to go along with it.' He stroked her hair and cupped his hands on her cheeks, loving the sense of belonging and *rightness* he felt. 'I want you in my life for ever, Abby. I want to wake up next to you and know that I'm coming back to you every day of every week of every year. I want you to have my babies. You make me complete.'

In receipt of that, Abby did what she had wanted to do since…for ever. She hugged him tight, wrapped her arms around him and he wrapped his around her, as secure and protective as the warmest of blankets, as steady as the most solid of rock.

She raised her face to his and smiled. 'I want all of that as well, so, yes, Gabriel. Yes, yes, yes! I'll marry you…'

EPILOGUE

THREE MONTHS LATER they were married in the little local church in the village where Abby had grown up. It was packed to the rafters. To Gabriel's bemusement, everyone from the butcher to the milkman was there to support them both.

'Now I know,' he murmured, halfway through the reception party, 'What it must feel like to be royalty. I'm surprised there wasn't a run on red carpets so that they could lay one down for us.'

She dazzled him. Seeing her walking up the aisle towards him had brought a lump to his throat and he had had to look away quickly to gather his emotions. The guy who had been proud to think that his heart was encased in ice had watched his beloved wife-to-be walk towards him and had wanted to cry.

Abby had laughed and told him that the paparazzi had nothing to do with her or anyone in the village. 'That's all for you,' she had teased, looking at him with a heart so filled with love, she thought it might burst. 'So, when it comes to being treated like royalty, look no further than yourself, my darling.'

The months leading up to the wedding had been hectic. Her parents had returned from their cruise, beyond excited to meet the guy who was going to be their son-in-law, and as expected Gabriel had laid it on thick with the charm. Afterwards, he'd told her just how nervous he had been.

He told her stuff like that now. The macho persona was still there but he no longer hid his emotions, at least from her.

'You're the other half of me,' he'd let her know. 'You get to see what no one else is entitled to see.'

Ava, of course, had been speechless with delight. The engagement ring, Gabriel had later confessed, had stayed in its box in a drawer in his bedroom.

'I couldn't tell her that it was off,' he'd confided. 'Somehow it would have felt too final and I suppose, deep down, I wasn't prepared to let you go. I just couldn't face a life without you in it. I just had to wake up to that fact, and thank God I did.'

They had a blissful two-week honeymoon on an exquisite island in the Caribbean and then, returning to England, they searched and found somewhere to live just outside London. A perfect cottage surrounded by fields.

A perfect cottage for kids.

And now...

Abby placed her hand on her still-flat stomach and smiled. They weren't yet in their perfect cottage and, when they *did* move in, it would be just in time for the addition that would turn two into three.

She heard the sound of the front door opening and she felt that familiar skipping thing her heart did whenever she saw him, whenever she *thought* of him.

Walking in, Gabriel dropped a kiss on her lips,

thought about it, deepened the kiss and kept kissing her as he kicked shut the door behind him.

Out of the corner of his eye, he could see that the table was set and there were candles on it.

'What's the occasion?' he asked, then he looked at her with dawning comprehension.

She loved the way he could do that—read her mind, predict what she was going to say.

'Nothing yet but definitely something in, oh, approximately seven months' time…' She grinned and tiptoed to kiss the side of his mouth. 'I'm pregnant.'

She took his big hand and guided it to her stomach and, for a few seconds, neither of them spoke.

Gabriel found that he couldn't. He was going to be a dad. Joy swelled through him and he closed his eyes.

'My darling,' he said unsteadily. 'That's the most wonderful news any man could ever hear. I love you so much.' He kissed her again gently. 'I used to be scared of handing my soul over to someone else. You have my soul. For now and for ever…'

* * * * *

COMING SOON!

We really hope you enjoyed reading this book. If you're looking for more romance, be sure to head to the shops when new books are available on

Thursday
28th June

To see which titles are coming soon, please visit
millsandboon.co.uk

MILLS & BOON

Coming next month

THE BRIDE'S BABY OF SHAME
Caitlin Crews

"I can see you are not asleep," came a familiar voice from much too close. "It is best to stop pretending, Sophie."

It was a voice that should not have been anywhere near her, not here.

Not in Langston House where, in a few short hours, she would become the latest in a long line of unenthused countesses.

Sophie took her time turning over in her bed. And still, no matter how long she stared or blinked, she couldn't make Renzo disappear.

"What are you doing here?" she asked, her voice barely more than a whisper.

"It turns out we have more to discuss."

She didn't like the way he said that, dark and something like lethal.

And Renzo was *here*.

Right *here*, in this bedroom Sophie had been installed in as the future Countess of Langston. It was all tapestries, priceless art, and frothy antique chairs that looked too fragile to sit in.

"I don't know what you mean," she said, her lips too dry and her throat not much better.

"I think you do." Renzo stood at the foot of her bed, one hand looped around one of the posts in a lazy, easy sort of grip that did absolutely nothing to calm Sophie's nerves. "I think you came to tell me something last night but let my temper scare you off. Or perhaps it would be more accurate to say you used my temper as an excuse to keep from telling me, would it not?"

Sophie found her hands covering her belly again, there beneath her comforter. Worse, Renzo's dark gaze followed the movement, as if he could see straight through the pile of soft linen to the truth.

"I would like you to leave," she told him, fighting to keep her voice calm. "I don't know what showing up here, hours before I'm meant to marry, could possibly accomplish. Or is this a punishment?"

Renzo's lips quirked into something no sane person would call a smile. He didn't move and yet he seemed to loom there, growing larger by the second and consuming all the air in the bedchamber.

He made it hard to breathe. Or see straight.

"We will get to punishments in a moment," Renzo said. His dark amber gaze raked over her, bold and harsh. His sensual mouth, the one she'd felt on every inch of her skin and woke in the night yearning for again, flattened. His gaze bored into her, so hard and deep she was sure he left marks. "Are you with child, Sophie?"

Continue reading
THE BRIDE'S BABY OF SHAME
Caitlin Crews

Available next month
www.millsandboon.co.uk

LET'S TALK
Romance

For exclusive extracts, competitions
and special offers, find us online:

f facebook.com/millsandboon

📷 @millsandboonuk

🐦 @millsandboon

Or get in touch on 0844 844 1351*

For all the latest titles coming soon, visit
millsandboon.co.uk/nextmonth